KNOTS

Chuck Boeheim

Lampworks Publishing

This is a work of fiction. All characters are products of the author's imagination and are not intended to represent any actual persons living or dead

To my feline writing companions
Tatterdemalion
Mayday
Lunatic
Bonkers
Rumplethumpkin
Yomogi

Contents

A Klein Bottle

The figure watched and listened in the shadows, far more patient than the slowly ticking clock. When many hundreds of ticks had fallen softly on the tapestried walls (two thousand, seven hundred and forty-nine ticks, this being the sort of person who counted such things), hearing no other sound than the mice who trafficked among the rushes on the floor, the figure left the shadows and entered the passageway opposite. He had a gem in his pocket that had formerly occupied a setting on a statue in the entry hall, but he sought a far more valuable prize in the lower levels.

He jumped at a sudden scrabble near the floor. He had nearly stepped on a mouse that was caught in a trap. Only its tail was caught and the little creature made short frantic lunges for freedom. He knelt to lift the jaw of the trap slightly to allow the tiny trembling soul its freedom.

He entered the passageway. The walls were covered with tessellations: repeating shapes that interlocked exactly, without gap or overlap. Each pattern was both art and math made real. The first tiles were simple polygons, then came Archimedean tessellations, which in turn gave way to more complex patterns. At each change of pattern on the surrounding walls, the figure stopped to identify and trace the set of shapes that created the repeating pattern. He knew he had traced each set correctly because he lived to attempt the next.

Between each section was a boundary of plain tiles. Automatically, he counted the tiles: eighty-one. He didn't count in the usual way; he knew their number at a glance without tallying each individual piece. This ability could be both boon and curse; it extracted its payments in various ways.

The corridor curved as it continued in an ever-narrowing spiral. In another place this would have been called a Fibonacci spiral, the shape in nature of a spiral shell or a hurricane or galaxy. This world, he had learned, had another name for it: a warding spiral. It kept those without from scrying what was within.

The figure came to the final section, no wider than his cloaked shoulders. The tessellation here was complex and non-repeating. A confident fingertip touched seven distinct shapes, then hesitated, sensing that something was wrong. After several tense moments of searching he found it: there was an eighth shape that was a slight variation on one of the others. He touched this one as well and breathed a sigh of relief. He paused to wipe a bead of sweat from his brow before turning to face the door at the end.

The door contained a mandala, a maze to trap the eye. Any adept who could solve the tessellation problems would feel an overwhelming compulsion to trace the mandala to its center. However there was a flaw in the maze that would keep such a person trapped here, ceaselessly tracing a line that looped back on itself. The figure produced a small vial from his cloak and extracted a small paintbrush from the vial. He reached out without looking and made the single stroke that repaired the flaw and disarmed the trap. Then he traced the line of the mandala from edge to center because it pleased him to do so, and because he could hardly have done otherwise.

Now he could consider the lock on the door. To the eye, it was a golden knot that floated on the surface of the dense wood of the door, a complex braid of energy that was bound by the crossings of the cord within it. While the Knot was whole, one could not touch the door and live. He studied the crossings carefully, then pulled several cords from his pocket that he had prepared in advance. He selected the one that had the best correspondence to the glowing braid and made a few small adjustments to it, then placed it next to the lock. When he used a small sharp instrument to snip one loop of his cord, the lock fell silently open. The cord vanished in a puff of smoke. Not having been turned into a scorch mark on the wall, he counted this as a success.

Now he passed through the door into the chamber within. Since the spiral passageway had gone through several complete turns and narrowed to the width of his shoulders, one would have expected the center to be a claustrophobic squeeze, rapidly becoming impassible.

One would be wrong.

He stepped into a chamber twenty paces across, hung with dark tapestries at intervals on the concave walls, and a dais in the center. The floor was a mosaic depicting the world in minute detail with tiles little larger than grains of sand. This was the world after the Great Geography Disaster, which had scrambled the map like a titanic jigsaw puzzle. The town of Plurs, which appeared to have once been a Swiss town, now had a bridge to Norway on the north, a gateway to a Spanish town on the west, a mountain pass to Mongolia on the east, and a trail to a village in the Amazon on the south. The town had a position on the map near the center of the room, with a likeness of this very castle on its northwest. He wondered if he knelt down to look in the windows of that castle whether he would see a microscopic version of himself within. Such things were possible here.

On the dais sat an object of impossible and luminous beauty. The object had a single transparent surface that curved gracefully back into itself in a figure 8 with a twist. It was an idealized Klein surface, with no inside and outside, and yet nowhere was the surface pierced. Enclosed by this surface was a bright Knot. According to the master of the castle, this Knot contained a portion of the magic released by the Geography Disaster and was stored here at its epicenter. This was more valuable to the thief than any jewel or artwork that he could steal.

With a finger that did not quite touch the surface, he traced the curves of the enclosure: in, out, around, and back to the starting point but upside down. One more complete circuit and he was back to the original point and orientation. At all points the bright Knot remained out of reach on the other side of the transparent barrier. He acknowledged to himself that it was a trick beyond his present abilities to create and not one that could be accomplished in only three dimensions.

He did not attempt to break the container. Even if he could be moved to break such a thing of beauty, he knew it to be futile. The twist that had been placed upon it had rendered it unbreakable, not unlike a Prince Rupert's drop without the vulnerable tail. Nor could he take the container with him—it was intertwined with the space around it; moving it would be like trying to carry the entire castle with him.

He removed another cord from his pocket, this one a true Knot of the twenty-fifth order, intricately crossed. As a true Knot (what the commoners called knots were merely braids), it was a continuous loop with no endpoint. He hadn't expected a Klein surface, and this Knot was not the right tool for the job. Still, he could improvise. He carefully cut one loop of the Knot, being meticulous not to fray the ends, and passed it around the container as close to the midline as he could. As he rejoined the cut ends, the Knot thrummed with power, giving him hope that it would work. He traced a pattern in the air above the Knot and it contracted into a glowing line on the surface of the container. As minutes ticked by, the sounds of strain came from both the cord and the container. He concentrated on his task, hoping the cord would be strong enough. With a soft popping sound, the cord imploded through the surface, and he breathed a sigh of relief. The bottle separated into two Möbius strips, one left-twisted and one right-twisted, which fell apart on the dais. Each was a clear loop that twisted once so that it had only one surface and one edge.

The thief reached quickly and incautiously for the prize. The left-twisted Möbius strip leapt up and bound his wrists together. *Of course it was the left-twisted strip*, he thought. Counter twists are always less trustworthy than forward twists. Why? Why was the universe made more of matter than antimatter? If there were reasons for either asymmetry, they had yet to be uncovered.

As he strained against the shrinking band, a tapestry on the opposite wall was flicked aside, and the master of the castle stepped into the room. He was dressed in his customary black shirt, breeches, and boots, with a red vest. In one hand he held a sword; in the other, he held a Knot of Captivity. His stance was impeccable and the blade had fine scratches and small nicks along its surface that attested to the usage he had given it. The thief could see in his eyes — storm gray under black slashes of eyebrows — that some of the nicks on the blade were undoubtedly earned by biting into human bones.

"This is poor repayment for hospitality given freely."

"I do agree with you, but you have something that I need." He didn't elaborate. This Knot was his way home, to a place where maps were not puzzles for mages to rearrange. His erstwhile host didn't strike him as the sympathetic type. He twisted his wrists, testing his bonds.

"Need? Or want?" demanded the master. "Why did you not simply make an offer for it, or ask for a boon?"

"Would you have parted with it for anything that I could have offered?"

"Not for anything anyone could have offered."

"There you have it. Why signal my intentions? Speaking of which, you are dressed and armed. It was no alarm that betrayed my intrusion here. What gave it away?"

"My necklace whispered it to me."

The thief's eye went to the chain of off-white links. "That thing of bones? It doesn't suit your style, you know."

"The bones from the inner ears of a few of my former enemies. They whisper when someone does not have my best interests at heart."

The thief involuntarily counted the seven hundred and twelve bones that made up the necklace and swallowed in apprehension. "How fortunate that you've completed it."

"I am now working on an amulet of dried eyeballs that will let me see what the next few minutes of my future hold. I need quite a few more for that endeavor, and I'm so glad that you've just volunteered to help." The master's eyes flicked to the Möbius strip binding the thief's wrists to assure himself that it held. He slid his sword into its scabbard and stepped closer as he spread the Knot of Captivity with a thin smile. "There are other parts I can use as well if I don't damage them with a blade."

The thief spat, expelling the fifth-order Knot of Confusion that he had tucked in his cheek. The Knot unraveled in a flash of light the moment it touched the master of the castle. The master threw the Knot of Captivity, but this landed several yards away from its target. The master drew his sword and swung but missed by an even wider margin. Every attempt to correct his course took him further from the thief. He roared in frustration.

The thief plucked a hair from his head and quickly knotted a counter-binding charm. He couldn't reach the band on his wrist, however, so he placed the counter-charm on the dais and laid his wrists on top of it. The Möbius strip loosened, allowing him to work his hands free. He seized the glowing Knot and stepped to the far side of the room. There, he drew a complex figure in chalk on the floor and lay down in the center of it, arranging his limbs so that the geometric pattern he had sewn to the inside of his garments aligned with and completed the pattern.

"Wait, oh clever one!" commanded the master of the castle. "Tell me at least the name of the one who has bested me. I am sure it is not the one that you gave at my door. Are you the thief that you appear to be, or does the great Game have a new player?"

Pausing for conversation was not a good idea, and the thief was not one to boast or taunt. He had done so before, to ruinous cost. The master of the castle was already learning to compensate for the distorted view the Knot of Confusion was feeding him, like looking through a prism that shifted the room by thirty degrees. He would be able to land a strike with that sword in a few seconds. The thief traced a quick formula in the air, an inequality that had only a small set of defined solutions.

"Your name!" insisted the other.

This was not a land in which names had power if indeed any such existed. Still, for much more mundane reasons it was not wise to give his real name. As the thief sketched the last term in the air to constrain the equation to a single solution, he began to fade from view. He found he couldn't resist a boast after all. He gave a false name, but one that claimed his signature skill. Too bad no one here would get the joke.

"Call me Escher," he said. And he was gone.

The glowing Knot hung in the air where his hand had grasped it, then dropped to the floor. It came to rest on the ancient city of Geneva, now situated in North Africa. The only magic at play here was that of irony.

Astromancer

The Plurs Chasm

September 4, 2018

Today, on the four hundredth anniversary of the Great Geography Disaster, it is worth remembering when the entire world began to shake as night fell over our city. Rocks fell from the sky, and landowners who had skimped on the sturdiness of their structures had cause to regret their miserly provisions when their buildings were the first to fall down.

Near midnight came a great roaring and the land pitched like the deck of a ship in a gale. It subsided after a period of hours, and with the dawn, people dug out of the rubble to greet a changed world. Gone were our neighboring villages and towns and the river that had flowed nearby. As reports continued to come in from farther away, our forefathers learned that even our constant companions, the mighty Alps, were no longer there.

New chasms divided the land into the remarkable geometrical sections that we have come to call geogons. When those chasms were eventually crossed, we found new lands on the far side, lands that had formerly been thousands of leagues distant.

The people of Plurs rebuilt, opened trade routes with our neighboring geogons, and soon thrived. We had an influx of new and diverse residents: French, Norwegian, Chinese, and more. We've been more fortunate than many lands that were overrun by hostile tribes, enslaved, starved, or worse. In our prosperity, we should never forget that the name Geography Disaster was well earned.

Two weeks prior

At the edge of town was an abrupt hill, a hill that seemed to have no reason for being where it was. It wasn't connected to a range of hills. It wasn't the forerunner of a rising landscape. It was a common monadnock, the sort that crops up everywhere when a bit of rock is more resistant to erosion than the surrounding land. Common, but nonetheless always surprising. It was no wonder that the local astromancer had built her tower atop it. Astromancy was held in the same regard in this world as astrology was in a slightly different world. It was kooky; it had no basis in observable fact; it produced no results that were distinguishable from random chance; and it had many fervent adherents. Nonetheless, the man who had called himself Escher had come to consult her.

The path to the top wound anti-clockwise around the hill, two and a quarter turns. There were seven lanterns along the way and twenty-two stone markers beside the path. Escher counted them automatically, compulsively, and made patterns in his head. He was bothered; it would have been much more pleasing had there been twenty-one stones. At the top, one hundred and seventeen flagstones lead to the structure. Restive wind chimes inhabited a low tree and shed silver notes over the path. The sun touched the horizon as he reached the door.

The tower resembled an eighteenth-century domed observatory that had been infested by outgrowths of crystal. The door was of a dark tropical wood; with the new geography of the world it could have come from as little as a few leagues away. A bell pull dangled beside the door; being expected, the man tugged the rope twice and heard a far-off clangor. A moment later, a voice issued from a grating beside the door.

"Please come on up. I am all the way at the top." The snick of a lock withdrawing was heard.

Escher entered and glanced back at the door. A cord ran up through the ceiling to allow the lock to be released remotely. He nodded. The stairs climbed around a rectangular stairwell, passing a few closed doors before one at that very top that spilled golden light into the dark stairwell. He ascended; there were eighty-three steps.

A small woman awaited him in the doorway at the top. "Good evening, Monsieur Chesrè." He had given an alias when he had requested the meeting, of course. "My apologies for not meeting you at the door, ha, but I cannot climb these stairs quite so many times in a day as I once could, ha ha. I am Lady Moonbird." She used a nervous laugh as punctuation, and her hands fluttered as she spoke. Escher wondered if she had adopted the name because of her mannerisms or the reverse. He looked around at the space, which had the look of having been decorated by an interior designer who had shopped at the garage sale of a Victorian astronomer. Upholstered chairs were grouped among instruments of brass and lenses. Eclectic did not begin to convey the effect of this jumble.

"Thank you for the appointment. I wished to consult you about …"

"Oh, no need to rush into business, ha, M. Chesrè. Please sit and have a cup of tea. Rest from your ascent up the hill. Enjoy the view that it has earned you, ha ha."

The man sat, resigned that the pace of life in this town was slower than that to which he was accustomed. He took a biscuit from a plate and dipped it in his tea before recalling that wasn't done here. Lady Moonbird sat across from him, sipping her own tea, chattering about her day in the garden, saying with gentle humor that the rabbits thought that she should plant fewer flowers and more lettuce. He knew this was professional patter; designed to ease her customers into talking about themselves. He let the words wash over him, only answering briefly as needed. Small talk was not his forte; he preferred witty repartee or silence. Later, he was unable to remember what they spoke about over tea, only that it had seemed entirely inconsequential.

As they set their teacups aside, Lady Moonbird said, "Well, M. Chesrè, let's cast your stars, ha, and see if we can find you a way home."

Escher looked up in astonishment from his activity of nudging the tea biscuits into intricate patterns on the table. He had only eaten one. "What makes you say that?"

"Hee hee. You've come to consult an Astromancer about your future and you're surprised I can see your present."

She dimmed the lights inside and cranked open a shutter high above on the dome. The central instrument in the room was a transit scope where lenses were mounted in an open framework. She swung the frame around to align it with a bright star overhead and applied her eye to a finder scope. Escher had never learned the conventional constellations, so he was unsure which star she was sighting. She moved some small thumbscrews for fine adjustment, then pulled a clutch. A clockwork movement began spinning slowly back and forth, driving gears that moved the scope to follow the star as it transited the sky.

Moonbird tilted her head as if listening to a message from the star in the crosshairs. "I see. You don't know the way back. But your question is how, not where."

Escher was shaken by her insight and was tempted to fabricate a story. But he had nothing to hide; if she saw that he was lying, he might not get the lead that he sought. So he went with the truth. "That's eerily accurate. One night I was crossing the Pont des Bergues in Geneva when a sudden fog came upon me. I couldn't see either bank of the river and all the noises of the city died away. I heard strange music, as of a harp playing. I held on to the rail to keep walking across a bridge that suddenly seemed much longer than it had been. I stepped into the Place du Rhône but lost my way within two strides. The fog cleared as quickly as it had come, and I was in the Square of the Jewelers here in the center of Plurs; there was no Geneva, no river, no bridge, and no lake anywhere to be seen. How do I find my way back?"

Moonbird placed a white gem in front of the lens, which amplified the starlight collected by the scope and split it into beams that reached out in many directions to touch the dome. She recorded the exact position in each constellation that a beam touched, and read a prediction from her charts. "Your journey starts at a castle outside of town." Escher noticed that she had lost the little laugh that she used for punctuation, and spoke with a firmer and deeper voice. "Go to the master's vault to find the way to your true home."

"What does he have that I need? And is he going to be willing to give it to me?"

Lady Moonbird placed a prism in one of the major beams emanating from the gem. This one beam split into three and fell on other asterisms in the sky. "Stealth. Misdirection. Danger. No, you cannot simply ask for this thing. Be circumspect and await your opportunity."

Moonbird lit a small gas lamp and put it in an enclosure that had only a pinhole for the light to escape. That light fell on a series of lenses and prisms that at first diffused the light, then focused and directed it as she turned small knobs. She aligned these light beams with those from the prism, and then engaged a gear. The enclosure was driven by another clock-work mechanism that very slowly precessed these beams away from their alignments. "For this journey, I will ask the heavens to grant you Courage, Trust, and Fortune."

"What do you mean you grant me these things?"

"Heh, heh, not me, dear, the heavens." She had shifted from her oracular voice back to her nervous tick. "Maybe your Astromancers were not so advanced as my guild, ha. We go beyond casting the fortunes of those who come to us. Hee hee! We nudge the stars, ever so slightly, to steer your fortunes in a favorable direction."

"I see," said Escher, trying to keep the doubt out of his voice. He had at least gotten the pointer that the old bookseller had said that he might. He now had to engineer an invitation into a castle. This was a task he knew well.

"Oh, one other thing, dear," said Lady Moonbird. "Be sure you know why you are on this path. Revenge is seldom as satisfying as we imagine, ha!"

Escher gave her a hard look, but she had already turned to the task of tidying up their cold teacups and biscuit crumbs.

After he had said good evening (and exchanged a discreet purse of coins), he made his way down the stairs again. There was still one too many marker stones on the path, and this still made him twitchy. Lady Moonbird had been very good at probing for information without seeming to; she had prattled about taking a trip home, and then later told a story of having the way home blocked by an accident of geography. He knew that he had reacted enough to both of those for her to form her guess, and then he had confirmed it himself by filling in the details. So her forecast was a sham, just like the astrologers at home. He was convinced that the patter about influencing his future was just as much malarkey as the forecast. Most of her clients would selectively remember random events that bore out her influence and forget those that didn't. Still, as long as the castle and its master was real, he had the lead he wanted.

He couldn't think of anything he had said that would have elicited that comment about revenge, however. He had been careful to keep that out of his mind during their conversation.

He put his hand in his pocket as he walked, and discovered that he came away with a magnifying glass that had lain on a side table in the observatory. He didn't remember stealing it, but that wasn't unusual. He often ended up with small items of uncertain ownership in his pocket.

Escher had entered the first empty streets when a clatter down an alleyway put him on his guard. Even the streets in this section of town were dark and narrow; the alleyways were places that even muggers feared to go. He looked for either shelter or a weapon and came up short on both commodities. He had a small knife but was unskilled in its use, and several Knots that were more suited to breaking and entering than armed confrontations. He braced himself as the tumult of upset trash bins and broken crockery issued from the alleyway in the company of a streak of gray fur.

Two hardened tomcats ran from the darkness with the lesser speed of those who own the territory and aren't afraid of anything else in it. Escher planted himself in front of them and waved his arms. "Scat!" The striped one that lacked both an eye and an ear on the left skidded as it backpedaled into the darkness it had come from. The orange tom with a disgusting case of mange tried to make a dodge around Escher to chase its adversary, but the pointed toe of a boot convinced it to change course and disappear into a hole in a fence.

"Thank you for stepping in. Do you mind if I walk with you a bit?"

Escher looked down at the smoky gray cat. "You talk?"

"I can do linear algebra, and you're hung up on the fact I can express myself in simple words?"

"Um, sure. There are some bits of fish left over from my dinner at home if you want to walk that far."

"Nothing else on my calendar this evening. I accept."

Escher continued home, followed by a new shadow. Perhaps this was the Trust that Lady Moonbird had forecast for him. It would do for now.

Tessalurgeon

The Plurs Chasm

July 1, 2017

A small geomantic realignment occurred in the early hours of the morning today. While many of the city's inhabitants slept through the event, those who felt it reported a mild rolling sensation, accompanied by the creaking of beams and the rattling of dishes. The Inn of the Cheeky Sparrow reported that an entire china cabinet tipped over, but authorities are placing the blame for that incident on a resident poltergeist that had been neglected.

Professor Salaun of the Department of Geomantic Studies described the event as 'minor.' Given the amount of time that has elapsed since the previous event, she said, there were likely to be additional realignments in the coming months.

The Border Patrol reports that all bridges leading out of Plurs still lead to the same geogons they have for the past ten years. There have been no reports of realignments of borders more than one geogon away from us, though it can take several days for reports to trickle in.

For now, our trading partners remain in place. Last night's event should still serve as a reminder that our neighbors can change at a moment's notice. The town council reminds everyone to be prepared for the next major realignment.

Trefoil prodded the still figure with one paw. The man who had called himself Escher groaned and attempted to rise from the circle inscribed in the stone floor. He made it as far as his knees before doubling over, head in hands. From the light coming in the windows, it had been several hours since the encounter in the castle.

"Had to use your escape hatch, eh?" said Trefoil.

Escher winced. "Please don't shout."

"I'm whispering."

"Still too loud."

"What's the matter with you?"

"I was hasty in drawing the figure. Some of the ratios must have been off slightly. Only slightly because I'm still alive. But I have a seventeenth order headache. And worse, I lost what I went to steal. I felt it slip through my fingers as I escaped."

"Why the haste?"

"I had no desire for my head to be parted from my body by a very sharp sword." His hands clenched as the headache throbbed. "Although, now I'm not so sure that wasn't the better alternative."

"I presume you were discovered?"

"I'll tell you about it if I live. I need to put an ice pack on my head. Is there anywhere to obtain ice?"

"Ice should be plentiful in, oh, about five months. I'll go get the tessalurgeon from down the street."

"No, wait!" But Trefoil had slipped away, in the manner of his kind.

Escher staggered to his feet, then hung on to a chair while the nausea passed. Crossing to a cold fireplace on one wall, he tried to clear his vision enough to see the tilework on the mantlepiece. Why did the puzzle have to be difficult today? He studied the tiles through the marching migraine lights that flickered in his eyeballs. He touched three tiles in succession then waited. The tiles shifted into a new pattern; he had missed the correct sequence. He tried again, but the moving lights had reached the center of his field of view, forcing him to use peripheral vision to see the pattern. His eyes wanted to track the pattern, trace the borders of the tiles, but every time he did, the tiles disappeared behind the migraine lights. He forced himself to look aside, to build up awareness of the interlocking pattern until he could grasp the answer. He reached out and touched four tiles, then a fifth.

The central keystone tile swung aside, revealing a space behind it. He put his lock picks within, both magical and physical, and the gem that he had managed to retain. That was scant consolation for missing his main prize, but he had needed a small theft to settle his mind for the primary goal. He would donate it to the Daughters of the Road later, to help them in their work. He closed the keystone tile and watched the puzzle reset itself to a new configuration.

He heard footsteps without, and voices. One of the voices belonged to Trefoil, the other he didn't recognize. He hastily pulled an intricately knotted carpet over the figure inscribed in the floor and sat down at the tallest of the four chairs drawn up at the table. He groped for the flask of water and poured a glass with trembling hands. The voices were now just outside the front door, on the path from the street. Escher closed his eyes for a moment to assure himself he had resumed his public persona. As long as life ran according to the scripts he had memorized, it worked reasonably well for him. It was much harder while suffering from a headache.

"After you," Trefoil said, from just outside. "For obvious reasons, I can't open the door for you."

Escher heard the latch turn, then recoiled from the painful blast of light that was admitted with his visitor. He threw his arm over his eyes. "Enter! Just shut the door quickly!" Squinting, he could barely see the form of a man, satchel in hand, with the shadow of Trefoil slipping in behind him.

"I am Edouard Scaldeforde, Tessalurgeon. You are Master Resche? Your, ah, associate asked me to come hastily." He was a gangly man, and it was evident that Tessalurgy had no cure for acne. His voice, at least, was soothing and calm.

"I have a sudden and very severe headache. Can you treat it?"

"It may be that I can. Sudden you say? Have you had these in the past?"

"Yes, it's a migraine. A bad one."

"I am not conversant with a grain headache. Can you tell me more?"

"Migraine! Migraine. Sudden headache with nausea, mostly on the left side, flashing lights in the eyes, moving steadily across the field of vision …"

"Ah, hemicrania malheur! I believe I can help you. Let me see …" Scaldeforde placed his bag on the table and rummaged inside. He withdrew a set of large cards and flipped through them. He turned one to the thief. "Any reaction?" The card had some simple convex geometric figures with five or more sides and no acute angles.

"No."

"How about this one?" He held up a new card of figures with acute angles.

The thief winced. "Makes it worse."

"And this one?" A card with concave figures of various geometries.

"About the same."

Scaldeforde flipped through the cards while muttering to himself, then withdrew one. "I want you to look deeply into this. Let your eyes go wherever they want to go. Ready? Go."

The thief tensed, recalling the trap he had only recently avoided. But Trefoil was here, prowling in the shadows. He would intervene if this simple doctor were not what he seemed. With a deep exhalation, the thief looked into the mandala on the card.

Eyes traced lines, lines captivated eyes. Any mandala would do that to one such as he, but this was not a typical mandala. This mandala did not lead gracefully into a zone of meditation. He tried to do as Scaldeforde instructed but had trouble focusing because of the aura that still dogged his vision. At a point where the flickering lights obscured the path his eye was tracing, he suddenly skipped to another path, moving in the opposite direction.

He had been to a chiropractor a few times, seeking relief. This was like the sudden snap of the neck, but deep within his brain. The migraine aura vanished, and he could see clearly again. He continued tracing the pattern, though bothered that it had become a left-handed spiral now. After a few more circuits, the pattern abruptly reversed direction again. He felt another snap. A feeling as of a cool breeze brushed against him, and he traced the rest of the mandala with his customary ease. He looked up, realizing that the headache was gone.

"A remarkable cure. Might I obtain a copy of that miraculous mandala?"

"Alas, no. Without the prior diagnostics to select the correct mandala, one could easily make the headache worse. In the most dire circumstances, it's even possible to rupture a blood vessel in the brain with the wrong pattern. This would be a fatal error."

"I see the necessity. I'm sure it's quite beside the point that your income derives from administering the treatment personally."

"Sir!" The tessalurgeon looked down his nose. "That would be a most unworthy sentiment for me to profess."

"I'm sure it would. I meant no disrespect. However, where I come from, there's something called a 'royalty.' This is an arrangement whereby the author is paid a sum whenever his or her work is used, read, or performed, even by someone else. I might be able to suggest a way that each use of your mandala results in a transfer of such a sum directly to your purse. Such a shame that this necessity for personal diagnosis precludes such an arrangement from being useful."

Scaldeforde's eyes grew shrewd. "We shouldn't be too hasty. Now that you prod me to think about it, it may be possible to package the diagnostic cards with the treatment cards to lead the sufferer to the correct selection on his own. I may even be able to re-draw the mandalas to be safer to use, with minimally lessened effectiveness."

"Very good. See if you can do that. I've been working on a way for a book to transfer a coin to the author on each use. I call it Eidetic Funds Transfer, or EFT for short. We can see if we can adapt it to your treatment cards. Come pay me a visit when you have something feasible and safe."

"I will! By Pascal, this is a happy chance that you had a headache today!"

"I wouldn't go that far, but we may have a profitable relationship in the offing. Speaking of which, would you please pay the good doctor, Trefoil?"

Trefoil leaped up on the table with a velvet purse in his mouth, which he dropped in front of the tessalurgeon. Scaldeforde had the grace not to overtly count the coins in his presence, but discreetly judged the heft of the purse as he tucked it away. "You are most generous. I am glad I was able to help you today, and I look forward to a mutually beneficial acquaintance. Good health to you, sir."

Scaldeforde let himself out. Trefoil remained on the table, studiously washing his face with one paw. After the door had closed and the footfalls had faded, Trefoil looked sideways at the thief. "What was that all about, eh?"

"I believe I may have introduced this world to both intellectual property and over-the-counter medicine. I am wondering if my name will be lauded or cursed for these things?"

Trefoil gave him a long stare. "Are you baiting him or fleecing him?"

Escher shrugged. "Maybe neither. His desire to profit from his cure rubbed me the wrong way. I'll see what he comes back with."

Daughters of the Road

𝕿𝖍𝖊 𝕻𝖑𝖚𝖗𝖘 𝕮𝖍𝖆𝖘𝖒

August 1, 2018

The Plurs Symphony begins its season this week with the return of Meisterin Aaltonen for her fourth year as principal conductor. She has kept the program fresh and vital each season, and we look forward to another year of her leadership. The Symphony has acquired a new harp, and she has promised to feature works this year that highlight the ethereal voice of this beautiful instrument.

The man who called himself Escher sat for a time after the tessalurgeon had left. The small plaque outside his door did indeed say "M. Resche, Scryer," and the doctor had addressed him in this manner. It was no more the name he had been born with than any of the others.

A slender cat sat on the table washing his face. His short fur was the color of hickory smoke, and there was a three-lobed white blaze on his forehead that gave him his name. When the cat finally paused in his grooming, the man addressed him. "Trefoil, what do you know of a Great Game?"

"I know that you back slowly away from any invitation to play unless you're either the best there is or you have a death wish. These are people who would tamper with the fabric of the world when they should be directing their energies to providing warm homes for the benefit of cats."

"Their game is dangerous?"

"Their founder — spiritual founder, that is, there weren't enough bits of him left over to found anything — caused the

Great Geography Disaster. I have heard that they lose a few Players every year, and it's even more dangerous to be a bystander. Interfere with them and they'll flay you alive and preserve your peeled pit in a Klein bottle so you can contemplate your folly for the next hundred years."

Escher thought back to the castle vault: the epicenter, the extraordinary Knot, the question asked by the master of the castle. "Of *course*, Lord Molendinarii would be one of their number."

"Lord Molendinarii? You attempted to rob Lord Molendinarii? Without making any provisions to feed me if you didn't come back? I thought you were a responsible human."

Escher shook his head. A talking cat was still a cat, after all. But now the talk of the Game made a connection that he had been struggling with for a year.

"Plurs. I have been trying to remember since I arrived where I had previously heard the name of this town. A long time ago in my world — four hundred years or so — a mountain collapsed beneath a small town, wiping it off the map. I believe the name of that vanished town was also Plurs. I think that was no landslide; I think it was the Geography Disaster, and it split this world from mine."

"Fascinating. What of it?"

"There may still be cracks between the worlds. If these Players are exploiting them, perhaps I should join their Game. I could wait my chance for a crack like the one that brought me here."

"My advice is to stay away from those people. Try to slip through the cracks they make and you'll end up as an infinitely long one-dimensional cosmic knot, spending eternity watching the universe's mainspring run down."

"Worried about me?"

"Only that you're the best meal ticket I've had in quite a while. Who's going to buy fresh whitefish for my supper if you get yourself turned into an illustration for the next issue of Topological Conjuring Monthly?"

"You have convinced me to watch my step. I still need to make some inquiries; I am beginning to suspect this Game is how I came to be here, and may be my only way back."

"Why do you want to go back to a place where cats can't talk?"

"I have unfinished business there."

Trefoil's ears twitched back at Escher's flat tone. "What are you planning to do?"

"Ask some questions — discreetly. Starting with why Lady Moonbird directed me to Molendinarii."

"The astromancer? What have you to do with her?"

"I've been researching the split between this world and mine, and an old bookseller told me I should consult her. I was just coming back from that visit when I rescued you, two weeks ago."

"I had everything under control, thank you. I wonder …" Trefoil stopped to lick his left paw nervously. "I wonder how she knew where to send you?"

"She didn't say. She pretended to read it from the stars."

"She might be part of the Game. That would be just like a Player, to send a thief to steal a game piece."

"I think I need to go back and have a word with her. I may have been set up, and that's something that I have very strong feelings about."

"I'll go with you this time."

"We'll leave at dusk. In the meantime, it would be better to not keep the trinket I stole from Molendinarii at home. It could conceivably have a tracer spell on it. I should liquidate it and donate it to our favorite charity."

Escher removed the gem from the safe and set off towards the avenue of the pawnbrokers, where he met a man who said his name was Edwards. The negotiation to turn the gem into cash was relatively straightforward, involving only a single alias and a tale of a formerly wealthy aunt who had entrusted him to liquidate some of her jewelry to support her dwindling domestic staff. Neither of them believed the story, but it was necessary to keep up appearances.

Then Escher continued to a quiet street where there was a quiet inn. In the lintel above the door was a red tile, and the name of the establishment was The Hibernian. Inside, he was recognized and greeted as M. Chesrè. The proprietor was a plump and red-haired woman named Cara, who had a lilt that put to rest any question of the authenticity of the name of the inn. Escher handed over the purse that he had just filled at the pawnbroker's, at which Cara broke into smiles.

"Oh, Monsieur! This couldn't have come at a better time. A caravan of Tsinganoi who are friends to the Daughters just arrived in town, conveying a dozen women. Two are staying on here and the rest are traveling onwards to find situations for themselves. We've been able to help twice the number of women this year because of your sponsorship." This loose organization — the Daughters of the Road — spirited women and girls away from abusive homes, imprisonment, and slavery, and found places that they could have better lives.

"It's you who does the amazing work, day in and day out. I'm just glad to make the small contributions that I can."

"They're anything but small to us. Come into the back room for a moment. The group that I told you about is working on learning some skills they'll need now that they're not simply a rich man's property. I know you'd like to see what your coins are doing for their lives."

Escher didn't really want to see the women. He wanted to know, from a safe distance, that he'd righted a wrong or given someone their life back. He didn't want to make it personal. He had tried to explain that to someone once but had been unable to find a way for either to understand the other's viewpoint. Some words just seemed to have different meanings to everyone else in the world. But Cara insisted, so he went.

Escher had naively thought that the skills Cara had referred to involved sewing and cooking. Not because he believed that was women's work, but because this world still had more such expectations than his own. Beyond the door, however, he found girls learning to add sums and keep books of accounting. Another was struggling with the language in a law book, while a third had an intricate mechanism disassembled on a table. Older women, and some men, were instructing and assisting the younger ones.

"Everyone, this is M. Chesrè. He is our largest benefactor. Because of his donations, we have places for you to stay and food for you to eat. We can rescue more of your sisters and daughters. Please say thank you to him."

All the girls rose obediently and bowed to Escher. "Thank you, sir," they chorused. Escher wished that he had sent the purse via a courrier, but he gathered his wits and put on his public persona.

"Please, don't thank me. I've only supplied some money. You are combining hard work with a desire for a better place in the world. Your life will become what you make of it, not what others decide for you. You do not need to conform to the limits set on you by small people who only wish to control others. Forget expectations and find the inner voice that tells you what you could do, what you will do if you work steadily towards that dream."

The girls bowed again, bewilderment on their faces. Then one — the one who had been reading the law book — stood straight. She looked Escher in the eye and said, "We will. We will bow no longer. But still, I thank you for your words and for that chance. We will make the best of it."

One by one, the other girls straightened up and repeated, "We will make the best of it."

"I don't know where that came from," Escher muttered to himself as the girls returned to their tasks.

"From the heart, M. Chesrè. It came from the heart," said Cara.

One of the girls came up to Escher. "What do you do, Monsieur?" she asked. "I would like to learn to do that too."

No, you wouldn't, thought Escher. "I, ah, am an … an art dealer. But you should do what you love to do, not what I do." This answer was only partially true since he mostly dealt in stolen art. It made him feel like a fraud after the speech he had just given.

The sweet sounds of plucked strings drifted through the room. Escher looked around to identify the source. A dark-haired girl was bent over a box with strings, with small mallets in her hands. The notes were … pleasing. Mathematical. A series of changes rung in 3:2 ratios. Escher was drawn to the quiet order of the sounds.

"What is that instrument?" he asked the player.

"It is a Harp of Pythagoras, Master."

"Don't call me that!" He took a breath and continued in a kinder tone. "You don't need to call anyone your master any longer."

"Yes, M— Monsieur."

He thought he should make amends for his brusque tone. "What is your name?"

"It is Mia K–. No, just Mia. I have no family name now." She plucked the strings once more, a sad sound.

The notes of the harp hung in the air, haunting. Escher felt that he had heard their like before, but in different circumstances. He wasn't one to listen to music for its own sake; it could send him into a fugue of counting notes and measures, or at the very least yank his concentration in unexpected directions. He couldn't place where he had heard this before, but it nagged at him.

"How did you learn how to play?" he asked the girl.

"It was part of my training with my sisters. I was the best with the harp." She blushed. "That was immodest. I learned how to play to entertain, and to serenade. I even learned how to make a demon dance."

"And now?"

"I love music and want to share it with others. I will see the Meisterin of the orchestra here and ask if I can play in her concerts. What a wonderful town you have here, where a woman can not only play in an orchestra but can actually lead it!'

"It has opportunities, yes, but it still has far to go. But I am glad you have this chance, and I'm certain that you have the talent to make the most of it." The girl smiled a shy smile, and Escher counted the hazards of another conversation as navigated. It wasn't until he had exchanged a few more words with others of the girls and with Cara and had escaped into the impersonal streets once again that it hit him where he had heard the strains of that music before. He had heard such a harp play the night he had walked through the fog from his world to this one.

Scrying

The Plurs Chasm

March 8, 2004 (from the archives)

The Border Patrol has reported lower traffic for the last two months. Farm exports are down, with fewer caravans making the crossing. No recent geogon shifts have occurred locally, but Free Agents who travel to the east have been delayed in returning, suggesting that some disturbance in that direction has disrupted travel. However, two caravans of tsinganoi have passed through, the first in twelve years. The mayor insists that rumors that this is a harbinger of hard times are baseless.

Sunlight spilled through the windows. The man named Escher startled awake. He had fallen in bed exhausted last night and hadn't awoken until what appeared to be late morning. He squinted for his watch to determine the time, but he had left it facing the wrong way. He started to throw off his bedclothes but stopped as his hand encountered something furry. And slightly wet. Something much smaller than a cat, which would be the most reasonable source of fur in such a place, though Trefoil had shown no inclination to turn domestic and sleep on the bed. It took a moment to recognize enough features to identify what it had been.

"There's a mouse in my bed!" In point of fact, it was a dead mouse, neatly opened up to display the insides, some of which had leaked out to stain the sheet red. "Trefoil!"

The smoke-gray cat sat on the table, looking pleased. "It's still fresh, too."

"Ugh. Take it outside to eat it."

Trefoil flattened his ears. "But … it's for you."

"I don't eat mice!"

Trefoil turned his head away to look at the wall. He swished his tail once. "You don't know what you're missing."

Escher began to realize this was a present, and Trefoil was hurt that he wasn't glad to receive it. "Sorry, buddy, people simply don't eat mice. Just like you don't eat Brussels sprouts. I appreciate the thought, though."

Trefoil swished his tail. "I've never owned a human before. Sorry if I don't know much about your care and feeding."

"Don't worry about it. You're doing a great job."

After a brief breakfast (which didn't include mouse for either of them), Escher prepared for a new customer by setting out his scrying tools. There had been a card left the day before while he was out on his mission of charity, requesting a scrying. The caller had left no name but said that he or she would return at the tenth hour the following day. The handwriting was clear and firm, without ornamentation, but it nonetheless had a certain elegance to it. Escher thought it was probably written by a woman, but certainly by a person who felt in charge. He was interested to see how the person matched the writing.

An hour later, there was a knock at the door. Escher opened it to find a slender woman who had both the height and the presence to look him in the eye. He noted that she was dressed conservatively, in a calf-length wool skirt, a high-necked white blouse with no more than a sensible amount of lace on the front, and a jacket in a classic cut that matched her skirt. Her black boots were of a practical cut, low-heeled for walking, and had been highly polished before the dust of the streets started creeping upwards from the soles. Escher had found that one could tell much about a person from their handwriting and their clothes.

"Welcome," said Escher. "I am M. Resche, Scryer. How may I help you?" He bowed as the woman entered. She scanned the room once before facing Escher. She had the sort of eyes that no detail would escape. The sort of eyes that could make him nervous.

"I have been trying to find a keepsake, a compass that my uncle left for me. He may have hidden it, or someone may have taken it, but it was nowhere to be found after his death last month. It would mean so much to me to recover it. I have been checking the town's pawnshops, and the last one suggested that I try your services."

"I will see what I can do," replied Escher. "Much depends on the properties of the object, and your ability to recall as many details as possible about it. Please have a seat, I've made some tea."

She perched at the edge of the indicated chair. "I will confess that I don't expect much from this consultation, but I have exhausted other avenues of inquiry. M. Edwards said that you were resourceful and have a knack for finding lost items."

"I see you have a sharp mind and a skeptical one. That's good; I work with scientific principles that need to be questioned and tested. I don't ask you to accept anything you can't verify."

"Very well, M. Resche, I'll play along. Where do we start?"

"Perhaps your name and a few details of the item would be good?"

"Is my name material in finding the item?"

"Likely not, but it would give me a more polite form of address than "hey you," and less cumbersome than 'the lovely lady occupying the chair opposite me.'"

That elicited a hint of warmth around his visitor's eyes. "I suppose that is convincing enough. My name is Mademoiselle Emeline Cigne."

"And what do you do, Mlle Cigne?"

"Please call me Emeline. Most people I work with know me by that name." Escher noted that she had avoided the question. He also got the feeling that she was trying to distance herself from her family name, even though she had given it. Perhaps a falling out with them?

"I hope the tea is to your liking," said Escher, trying a different gambit. "I was always more of a coffee drinker."

"I don't believe I've ever heard of coffee."

"Alas, no one here has, so I must learn to like tea."

"You are from far away, then?"

"Yes. If you don't know of coffee, then you won't have knowledge of the place, either."

"Perhaps my uncle would have. He traveled quite extensively."

"This is the uncle with the compass, whom we can no longer ask?"

"The same. Do you have a name other than Resche?"

For a heartbeat, Escher thought she was inquiring about his alias, then realized that she wanted his given name. "Er, Maurits. But I don't often use it. And this compass, was it something he brought back from his travels?"

"I have always thought so, but I am not sure where it came from. It has a brass case with a hinged lid that has a miniature sextant built into it. There are some sighting posts, and some fiddly little knobs to adjust it to show both magnetic north and true north. My uncle showed me how to use it to find my way through a wilderness one time when I accompanied him on a short trip."

"It sounds like a classic compass, such as was used in ship's navigation." He was building up a profile of his customer to help fill in any details that the scrying left vague: most likely the daughter of a merchant family, moderately well off, able to afford those clothes and his fee. The wool skirt was both local and practical. Nobility would have worn garments of cotton, which had to be imported expensively from India, which was even further away in this world than it would have been in Escher's.

"Probably quite a common instrument. The only value is sentimental. My uncle meant for me to have it, and it recalls for me the stories he used to tell."

Escher wished that he had equipped himself with a Knot of Veracity, but even lacking one, he felt that on this point she was deviating from the truth.

"Then let us begin," he said. "I will prepare the scrying vessel." There was a silver bowl on the table, which he filled with water. He placed a teacup beside it and filled it as well. He knotted a cord into a figure with five crossings and bound the two loose ends together. He draped the cord over the edge of the bowl, so one end was in the bowl and the other in the teacup. Emeline leaned forward to watch his preparations with interest.

He produced another cord. With this, he fashioned an intricate figure of seventeen crossings. He turned and placed this in Emeline's hands. "Please gaze deeply into this Knot and form the most detailed mental image of the compass that you can. Imagine that image sinking into the Knot and becoming entangled with it. Make the compass as solid in your mind's eye as the Knot is." She complied, but Escher could see the wariness in her eyes. She was trying to figure where the sleight of hand would be. He could sympathize; he had done the same with Lady Moonbird. The difference was that scrying worked.

By now, the teacup had steam rising from it while condensation formed on the rim of the silver bowl. He waited for another minute until the water in the teacup was starting to boil, and a rime of ice was just beginning on the bowl. He gingerly lifted the string that had bridged the two vessels with the tines of a fork, since it was now uncomfortably warm from the work of transferring heat from the bowl to the cup. Its job done, the string vanished.

"Keep concentrating on the Knot," he instructed. As he blew gently across the surface of the teacup, a stream of mist began to condense above the silver bowl. After one minute, he had a shifting cloud hanging over the bowl. After two, the mist had settled into a dense lake of fog, lapping at the edges of the bowl.

He held out his hand without looking. "Let me have the Knot now. Move slowly so that you don't make any breeze to disturb the mist." When he felt the Knot placed in the palm of his hand, he moved to hold it over the bowl. He could already feel the Knot stirring with the compulsion to move in the direction of the thing that was sought. He inverted his hand and let the Knot fall into the bowl. It disappeared into the lake of mist with a single puff, leaving a soft-edged impression of the intricate crossings of the Knot. Emeline made a small gasp, and Escher knew this would be a good scrying. When the Knot pulled the image of the desired object from your mind, it tickled somewhere deep in your brain that didn't know how to deal with being tickled.

The mist in the bowl began to swirl and churn. Soon it spilled over the side of the bowl on one edge, falling to the surface of the table. It collected there, then a thin trickle began streaming across the tabletop. At first, it meandered, then it became more confident in its direction. The trickle widened to a stream. Soon a river of fog crossed the table, fell to the floor, and headed towards the north. It got no further than the outer wall, but they had a long, straight baseline for determining the direction.

"Amazing," breathed Emeline.

"Just a moment while I get the map," said Escher. "We can plot the line this would take through town and see if it intersects anything interesting."

He had just started to turn for the map when he heard a sharp intake of breath from Emeline. Turning back to the table, he saw an image had appeared in the mist. It was a shelf, arranged like a display case. On the shelf were several brass instruments, the centermost of which was a brass compass, which matched exactly Emeline's description of the missing keepsake. It wavered for a moment, then was gone in the dissipating fog.

"Now, I truly am astounded," said Emeline. "I must admit that I'm professionally skeptical and didn't expect much from your parlor trick. However, that was most definitely my uncle's compass."

"I still find it amazing, no matter how many times I see it," said Escher smoothly. In truth, he was shaken. He had never conjured an image from scrying before in his career. He had counted himself lucky to get the direction of the object.

He found the map and laid it on the table, along with protractor and compass (the sort for drawing arcs, not the sort for finding north). He transferred the line on the floor to the map with precision, and they both leaned their heads over the map. Escher was conscious of a warm fragrance as they stood together at the table.

After studying the intersections of the line with the streets of the town, in which thirty-seven possible shops and residences were marked as potential locations, they both stepped back and shook their heads.

"I don't see any candidates that seem exceptionally likely," said Escher. "Though we can probably rule out a few of them. Johnson's Livery or the Chandler seem unlikely places for this item to be."

"I agree," said Emeline. "That leaves quite a few places to inquire. Still, it's better than I had before I came here today, so I am quite in your debt for what you've done."

"A moment, please. An exhaustive search shouldn't be necessary. We can repeat the scrying at another location to obtain a second line. The intersection of those two lines should narrow it down to a single place, or at most one or two neighboring locations."

"An excellent thought! How shall we do this?"

"We'll need another location some distance away, quiet, with still air. Let me think."

"Would my office suffice? There should be room enough for you to duplicate the arrangement you used today." She handed him a card.

"That should suit the purpose. Would you be available at the tenth hour tomorrow morning?" He glanced at the card and kept his face impassive. It took an effort.

"That will work admirably. Until tomorrow morning, then." She turned and found Trefoil sitting on the table, regarding her with an unblinking gaze.

"Good afternoon, M. Chat. I saw you watching me earlier. Have you come out to say hello?" She held a hand out to let Trefoil sniff her for a moment. Then she extended one finger to gently scratch him on the side of his face. After a moment, he turned his head and leaned into the scratching. Escher noticed that she gave Trefoil his space, and didn't take any unoffered liberties. She knew cats.

Emeline took her leave. Her footsteps on the path outside were measured and confident.

"She's not what she appears," said Trefoil.

"You didn't see her business card. She owns the town newspaper; I'm to meet her at that establishment tomorrow morning."

Observatory

The Plurs Chasm

November 12, 2017

Last evening, the Mayor put before the Town Council a plan to resurface Town Hall plaza. This plan would encompass taking up the old paving stones, regrading the area of the plaza, installing new stonework, replacing the existing fountain with a new design to be commissioned from the town's artisans, and the installation of marble benches and planters to divide up the area. It was even proposed that oriental fish could be obtained for the fountain. Plans were drawn up by the brothers Marmion, who are also the proposed contractors. All council members who were present spoke in favor of the project, citing the need to make the plaza a more fitting environ-ment for the seat of our government.

Dusk was gathering as the man named Escher ascended the path to the observatory. There were still seven lanterns and twenty-two marker stones on the path, and the number still bothered him. Trefoil ghosted just ahead of him on the path.

As they approached the observatory itself, they saw that the door stood open. The lock was broken.

"That's not a good sign," said Trefoil.

"It's not. You'd better stay back here. This may not be a good place for small cats."

"You're not very good at herding cats." Trefoil slipped past Escher's legs and darted up the stairs, fur puffed out to twice his normal size. Escher hurried after, torn between silence and haste. Eighty-three steps. An irritating number. The cat reap-peared before Escher reached the top.

"Don't go in. We're too late."

"You're not very good at herding humans." Escher pushed the door open, cautious of traps and assassins. Whoever had visited had not waited, however. The sad heap beside the table where Escher had drunk tea, two weeks earlier, was all that remained. Escher rolled her over, no longer so bird-like, seeming at once smaller and heavier than she had in life. Anger and fear mixed in Escher's intestines. Molendinarii had not been bluffing about collecting the eyes of those who crossed him.

Self-preservation urged him not to linger; he heeded that urging rather more quickly than he would have on a prior night. Escher hastened down the stairs, which descended in a series of flights around a rectangular well. He stopped abruptly on the eighty-fourth step. The end was still far below, and the tower door equally far above.

"Trefoil, there were only eighty-three steps going up. Wait here a moment."

Escher descended four more flights — one circuit of the stairwell — then looked over the side. The grey cat sat on the underside of the step, upside down from his viewpoint.

"This is probably not the time to show off tricks that are better left to squirrels," remarked Trefoil.

"Would that it were my trick," said Escher. "Stay there." He continued down the stairs. After four more turns, he once again encountered Trefoil, this time oriented in a less distressing direction. He had never stopped descending, but he nonetheless found himself arriving on the same step.

"We're in a perspective trap," he told the cat. "Molendinarii wanted anyone who came here detained until he returned."

"Or he simply wanted to keep someone from raising the alarm too quickly," suggested Trefoil. "Perhaps you can find a rope to climb down?"

"There's nothing to tie it to here. Let's see if we can return to the top of the tower."

After climbing only forty-four steps, they emerged into the observation dome once more. The space was filled by arrangements of lenses and small light sources that were familiar from his prior visit. A grouping of stars was visible through the slit in the dome, and the main optics were aligned on a prominent red star within it. Other lenses on clockwork movements directed beams of light towards stars and planets that Lady Moonbird had believed could influence events on Earth.

None of that helped him now. Even if there had been a shred of evidence supporting the practice, none of its claimed benefits included escaping from a sixty-foot tower. Faced with a sharp sword — or worse, scalpels — he would risk the drop. He searched for alternatives to that choice.

"I didn't reset my Congruence Circle, so I can't use that to transfer us back home. Probably a bad idea anyway, if Molendinarii learned my address from Lady Moonbird. He might be there waiting for me. Use a Perspective manipulation to walk down the side of the tower? No, the geometry's not right for that. Any ideas, Trefoil?"

The cat didn't answer. Looking around, Escher saw that he was sitting in front of the clockwork governor, a mechanism with four weights on the ends of rods that was spinning lazily. As it spun, the weights gradually lifted away, pressing pads at the top ends of the rods against a stationary ring, slowing the mechanism until the weights fell back. Correctly adjusted, this kept the speed of the mechanism regulated, so that the telescope above would track the slow movements of the stars across the sky. Trefoil was fascinated by the moving brass parts.

Escher traced the shaft to a gear with nine teeth. That drove a larger gear with 78 teeth fixed to a smaller one with 13 teeth, which drove another with 90 teeth. That last gear would revolve once for every 60 turns of the main shaft ...

He shook himself. No time to get caught up in the pleasures of counting and calculating. But there was something here ... His eye went the other way, where a cable was wound neatly around a shaft. The cable disappeared through a hole in a plate in the floor.

Escher opened the plate to reveal a heavy weight suspended below. Falling, it powered the clockwork mechanism. It had recently been wound and was not far below the level of the floor. "Trefoil, I found our way out."

Escher removed one of the Knots from his pocket and arranged it over the governor wheel. Then he returned to the cable holding the weight.

"That's never going to hold you," fretted Trefoil.

"Aren't you the optimist?"

"I'll have you know that cats invented optimism. Humans were such a gloomy bunch until we taught it to you."

"If you're an optimist, then you should be positively sanguine about our chances of making it to the bottom in one piece."

"What do you mean, *our* chances?"

Escher slid down the cable to stand with his feet on the weight. "Come sit on my shoulder."

"Oh, no. I don't ride. I'm not one of *those* cats."

"What will you say when the killer comes back to find you here?"

"Mew?"

"You can either take your chances with him or with me."

Reluctantly, Trefoil padded over to the well and stepped down onto Escher's shoulder. Escher pulled the cover back over the well, then crouched on the weight and drew out a Knot that was twin to the one on the governor. He pulled on one loop of the Knot, drawing the remainder of the Knot tight. The other Knot tightened simultaneously, shearing through the arms of the governor. With no braking action, the cable began to pay out faster. The weight picked up speed.

"Hang on!" called Escher as the whine of the gears rose in pitch. Their speed increased, and the feeling of a dropping elevator afflicted their stomachs. "I hope the gears don't shatter or burn up!"

"A fine time to think of that!" yowled Trefoil.

They weren't in free fall — far from it — but the wind of their descent billowed Escher's cloak. Trefoil hung on in the way of his kind, bringing a protest from his perch. "Watch the claws!"

"You said to hang on! Did you think I had opposable thumbs?"

The weight bounced to a stop at the end of its chain, causing Escher to yelp again as Trefoil scrambled to stay on. They hung about ten feet from the bottom of the well, oscillating slowly. Escher climbed down to hang from his fingertips from the weight and dropped the rest of the way to the ground. Trefoil jumped to the ground and sat grooming his shoulder with great care and attention as he got his nerves under control.

Escher tried the door and found it locked. It was a simple lock, and a third-order Knot of Unbinding opened it quickly. This let them into the central stairwell at ground level, where the exterior door still stood open. Escher re-locked the clock-room door and left the exterior door as they had found it.

Soon they were outside and heading down the path. The lanterns were burning low as dawn approached; there were still seven lanterns and twenty-two marker stones. Midway down, he stooped, picked up a marker stone, and tossed it down the hillside. In this small improvement to balance and proportion, at least, he felt better.

Through the slowly stirring town they made their way, following a route that took them wide of their street of residence to come back from a different direction, in case unfriendly eyes were watching. They entered the bakery on the corner from the side street and peered out the front window. Escher traded a coin for a sweet bun to maintain a pretense of an early morning stroll for breakfast.

"The fishmonger is open as well. Why couldn't we have stopped there instead?"

"That might look suspicious, this early in the morning. Do you see anything unusual?"

"Not at the moment, but the baker's cat says that someone was there earlier."

"How much earlier? Was it when Mlle Cigne visited me yesterday, or more recently?"

"He didn't know. He's not much more than an alley cat. If it's not a mouse, he's not terribly interested, and he can't even tell time."

Escher waited until the baker went into the storeroom for a moment then slipped through the door that led to the roof. He had been there once before when the baker had shown him his roof-top herb garden, which he kept for seasoning some of his breads. Escher knew that it had a good view of his front door.

He wanted to watch for a while to decide if it was safe to return.

He opened the door at the top of the stairs and stepped through. Trefoil remained on the stairs to watch for the baker.

A cold blast of wind blew him back against a rock face. In front of him, a cliff plunged thousands of feet onto jagged rocks. The horizon was gashed by mountains that were home to glaciers and snow cornices that promised swift burial of any who assailed them. The trail that he was on hugged the side of his mountain, leading to a dark keep brooding over the valley. Of the door through which he had just passed, there was no sign.

Cube Challenge

The Plurs Chasm

November 14, 2017

An investigation by reporters from the Chasm has revealed that the company proposing to renovate Town Hall Square is financially backed by the town's treasurer. The Mayor and most of the Council members are investors in that company as well. An emergency meeting of the Council following this revelation was preempted by a mob of angry citizens demanding accountability from their elected officials. When the police were summoned, the Chief of Police directed them to keep order and to refrain from violence but refused to follow the Council's demands to remove the protesters. In an interview outside of the Council chambers, the Chief said, "The police force works for the Magistrate, not the Council. They cannot order us to break up a legal assembly. Their job is to listen to the public, and if we removed the public we would prevent them from doing their job. That wouldn't be right, would it?"

The editorial staff of the Plurs Chasm heartily agree.

It took several minutes for the man with the uncertain name to conclude there was no doorway in the rock. His fingers were becoming numb, and it was evident that his only choice was the pathway to the keep. He was certain that was intended, as was his appearance outside on the ledge rather than by some nice cozy fireplace inside. Someone wanted an audience with him but wanted him in the proper frame of mind first. The pit of his stomach told him that they were probably succeeding, but he didn't have to let on. He put on his thief persona and faced towards the castle. That was his bravest persona, and right now he needed to convince himself that he wasn't afraid.

He began walking. Of course, he counted the steps. He was thankful that there were too many snowflakes to even consider counting. His compulsion drew the line at a level that couldn't be called sensible but could be called survivable.

The door of the castle was of heavy timbers bound with iron straps. It was locked. Escher looked for a puzzle or a mathematical curiosity that would unlock it. He was beginning to shiver, and his hands would soon be too cold to manipulate any of his knots. He wasn't even able to find a keyhole to attempt a lock-picking manipulation. The door was an obstacle, not a challenge. He began to seriously consider the possibility that he could freeze to death.

"No, not an obstacle, either. It's a message." There was a door knocker in the form of distinctly male anatomy. He grasped the part that was obviously meant for grasping, lifted, and let the weights fall against the striker plate. A sound of doom echoed inside. The door swung open. "So you have a pair of brass balls and you want the world to know it," muttered Escher to cover his relief. He entered.

Inside the door was an entrance hallway with a flight of stairs ascending at the end. A clock was ticking, recalling the one in Molendinarii's castle. A worn carpet was on the floor, and a woodblock print hung upon the wall, depicting a cube hanging in space in three-quarter perspective.

Escher began to climb the stairs. They were wide, with shallow stone steps. There were windows on each side, but the scenery within was simply painted on the stone walls. They were fake window frames enclosing artwork. Disturbing artwork. The scenes looked out upon evil woodlands with deformed creatures that lurked half-hidden, or burning wastelands in which giant creatures of fire drove blue-skinned humans like cattle, or a dark dungeon with chains dangling from the walls, with only a dismembered arm hanging from one to show they had been in use. As he ascended, the steps narrowed and grew steeper, each tread requiring a higher step. As the walls closed in, the windows became smaller, the images within painted in smaller scale. Escher had an overwhelming feeling that he was growing taller, becoming a giant in a dollhouse. By the time he came to the end of the unexpectedly short stair, he had to bend double to fit through the doorway.

"I feel like Alice after a bad mushroom," he said to the air. In case anyone was listening — and he felt sure someone was — he kept up his bravado. In truth, the owner of this castle had demonstrated power beyond anything he had seen before, and he knew that he had to keep his wits about him. But his hands were cold, and it wasn't just from the outdoor jaunt.

On the other side of the door, he could once again stand upright, to his great relief. This room was built to a normal scale. It had three doorways, one to his right, one straight ahead, and one, disconcertingly, in the ceiling. Through the doorways on his level were other, identical rooms. Through the doorway on the ceiling was yet another room, twisted ninety degrees. The wall to his left was white marble, the wall behind him was red stone, and the floor was of green slate.

One direction looked as good as any other. Escher turned right and went through the doorway. This room had doors at opposite ends of the room and one in the ceiling. Immediately there came a gray-white noise, a noise with no spectrum but with great weight, the sound of polished stones sliding against each other. Overhead, the room spun away and another room took its place. That one had one wall of yellow marble, while the one that had spun away had had one of blue granite. The room he was in had one wall of green slate and a floor of polished onyx.

"You've got to be kidding me. A giant Rubik's cube?"

He walked back into the first room. As he had expected, the small door through which he had entered was gone. The sound of moving stones came again, but instead of the reverse movement occurring overhead, he felt the room that he was in moving forward and up until he was standing at ninety degrees to his previous position, and two tiers higher. Fortunately, gravity shifted with him and he remained stuck to the wall.

"Right. The cube is obviously scrambled. It would be logical to think that the way out of the maze is to solve the cube."

Escher walked back and forth through doorways, noting which rotation was triggered by each movement, and building up a mental map of the current configuration of the faces. Of course, this constantly changed as he moved and the faces rotated in response. This was where his obsession with shapes and numbers turned into an asset. He soon knew every face and how to move them.

He started lining up the colors on each edge. He had once been able to solve a cube in under a minute, but this puzzle had constraints. He had a choice of only two rotations with each move because the overhead door was out of reach. He tried jumping up to catch the edge of the door but was a foot or more short. This was going to take far more moves than a hand-held cube. Steadily he aligned the colors, only to break them apart again when starting on the next. At every step, he planned the moves so that the final twist both aligned the current face and rotated the previous one back into place. He started breaking a sweat with the effort of jogging into room after room, and keeping his balance when the floors tilted from time to time. He had become totally absorbed in the challenge for its own sake and had stopped narrating his progress for his unseen host. He did wonder whether he would be better off not solving it; would it make him seem more useful or more of a threat? Either way, he could not help but continue. He had never been able to turn down a puzzle.

At last came the final pass. The faces were almost complete, but one corner was rotated one turn clockwise. He began the series of moves that would shift the corner around, rotate it, shift it back, and restore all the other faces to their current state. He was almost dancing through the moves to keep the puzzle in motion. The almost-order of the puzzle disintegrated into chaos as he started the transformation. He tracked all of the pieces in his head, watching them move into new constellations. There was the twist to rotate the errant corner. Now everything was flying back together, edges aligning, faces matching up. One more move—and it was one he had been dreading.

The only way to get the final rotation he needed was to drop through a door in the floor and plunge all the way to the opposite corner.

He reviewed this final move with great care. If he muffed it, he could break an ankle, if not his neck. As he passed through the first door, the room would start to rotate *this* way, and after he passed through the second door it would swivel *that* way. Steeling himself, he dropped through the doorway, but caught the edge of the door and held on for a count of five as the sound of sliding stone started. He let go and dropped, skidding along the wall that was turning into a floor, then standing as he slid through the second door and swinging to the side to stick his landing on the far wall, just as it changed its orientation from vertical to horizontal. He was gratified to see the door in the outer wall slide to a halt in front of him, and then open into a lavish chamber.

He emerged from the maze, flushed and still breathing hard. This new room was an opulent salon, with a massive fireplace on one side warming the room, tapestries and portraits and antique weapons decorating the walls. Several canvases depicted — in disturbing detail — hideous demons in the act of ravishing both men and women.

A reclining divan near the fire was occupied by a beautiful and regal woman, who resembled a number of the portraits on the wall. Her skin was a rose gold that he had never encountered before, making him wonder where she was from or by what means she had acquired it. Her gown was a diaphanous green, intended as accent, not concealment, for it concealed virtually nothing. Raven tresses tumbled over her shoulders, and a pendant with a large ruby lay in the shadows between her breasts.

"Bravo, mysterious stranger." She had a lilt to her accent that suggested the Iberian peninsula to Escher. "You have navigated my maze and come into my parlor, and, I might add, a good deal faster than many who came before you. You even appear to have enjoyed yourself in doing so. Who is this figure who has intruded upon our little Game?"

Escher felt a small disquiet at the number of people who had seen beneath the surface of his persona lately. Did he want to play the suave thief again, or would she see through it? He didn't have a better option ready. He bowed deeply and said, "You may call me Escher."

"I heard you told Molendinarii the same name as you left his presence, though it is but a *nom du vol*, is it not? One that you use for your surreptitious pursuits?"

"My true name has little meaning here, so it pleases me to use the name of a man that I admire. And whom do I have the very great pleasure of addressing?"

She smiled a warmly seductive smile that was somehow as chilling as the storm outside her castle. "I am the Contessa Hesperia."

"My Lady of the West," he acknowledged, connecting the lilt of her words to the name the Romans had once used for the lands that were — formerly — in the direction of the setting sun. "I had no intention of intruding on your Game. I was but interested in a trinket that Lord Molendinarii was reputed to have, which would further my efforts to return to my home."

"So that was your origin," said Hesperia slowly. "I thought as much. I don't mind that you discommoded that old schemer with your theft. It has added an interesting twist to the Game." Escher realized that Hesperia believed his theft had been successful. He said nothing, hoping he could turn it to his advantage. "I should just caution you not to try anything similar here. I have ways of dealing with those who try to steal from me."

"Do I dare ask?"

"Bits of them end up adorning my castle in interesting ways, serving, for instance, as a door knocker to warn others away."

Escher paled. "He, um, seems to have died … happy."

"His last moment was exquisite. A shame he doesn't remember it."

That would be easier news to take calmly if Escher hadn't been certain from the moment he entered the chamber that Hesperia possessed a Knot of geomantic power at least the equal of Molendinarii's, encapsulated in the ruby that lay against her breast. A perilous place to plan a heist.

Lady of the West

𝔗𝔥𝔢 𝔓𝔩𝔲𝔯𝔰 𝔆𝔥𝔞𝔰𝔪

February 12, 1996 (from the archives)

The people of Plurs were overjoyed this week at the return of an expedition that had departed over two years ago. Lead by the legendary Piers Cigne, the group of explorers had visited nearly a hundred geogons before finding the lost land of Ceylon. The way, which remains a closely-guarded secret, has closed off the island from commerce for centuries, since shortly after a colony was established there by the former nation of Portugal. The intrepid explorers were nearly lost on their return, as shifting geogons threatened to close off their way. But return home they did, bearing a load of cinnamon that is estimated to be worth five times its weight in silver.

"Please, take some refreshment after your exertions." Lady Hesperia waved towards a second divan nearby. The man who called himself Escher moved cautiously to take a seat. He found that he must either recline on the cushions at full length, as Hesperia was doing, or perch on the edge, stiffly. Did one recline in the presence of a Contessa? What message did he want to convey? He was unfamiliar with this calculus. He perched, stiffly.

"Try some of the honey dates," urged the Contessa. "They are most amusingly accented with cinnamon."

Escher selected one of the morsels from the table near him and placed it in his mouth. It was sweet, cloyingly so, just saved from intolerably sweet by the bite of the cinnamon. He also wondered what to do with his now-sticky fingers. "They are delightful," he said gallantly, if less than truthfully. "Where do you get dates on this snowbound mountain?"

"This castle is large," she said. "Not all of the doors open on a windswept mountain. Here, let me pour you something to slake your thirst." Hesperia arose and poured an amber liquid from a graceful ewer. She offered it to him, leaning dangerously forward. He kept his eyes on her face. She had succeeded in putting him off balance with her sexuality, but he was catching on, somewhat belatedly. It was all glamour and distraction, and he needed to find a way to turn it to his advantage.

He took a sip from the cup. It was the nectar of apricots, with the addition of some exotic spice that he couldn't identify. It might have been refreshing by itself, but after the cloying assault of the date, all he could taste was sweetness piled on sweetness. He drank for politeness's sake and set the cup aside.

"What can you tell me of this Game you play, Contessa? I've no desire to disrupt your play or inadvertently cross someone whose good favor I may someday need. But I am a relative stranger here and would like to know of the powers who are playing, and what their objectives may be."

Hesperia gave a laugh like chimes in the wind, light and free. "I'm sure you would. But one of the principles of the Game is the concealment and discovery of knowledge. I would tell you only what I know that might further my goals, or mislead others. And this round of the Game has just begun. There is much left to discover at this stage."

"But I am not part of your Game," protested Escher.

"You have become a part, though you may not be a Player. Or at least as far as I know. I have only discerned a few of the Players in this round as of yet. You may be a new Player, intent on misleading us by pretending you are not. Or another Player may have enticed you into involvement. Think on where your information has come from and what that person's motives may be. The mind that solved my entry maze is one that would enjoy this Game."

"How long have you been a Player?"

A small smile visited her lips. "Of all the things that should not be revealed, a lady's age is among the foremost."

"Um, right. I didn't mean it that way. Let me just ask if you were a Player in the last Game, a year ago?" She was keeping him off-balance; he reminded himself to stay in character.

"Certain information I am willing to give you for free, other knowledge must be traded for."

"I see." Escher wondered what he might have to trade. He became aware that he was still holding his sticky fingers awkwardly, not wanting to leave prints on the Contessa's furniture, or on his own clothes. "Do you have a basin in which I might rinse my fingers?"

Hesperia arose and crossed the space between the divans. Escher told himself to count the beads on her collar, the facets on her ruby — no, that was not a safe direction to look. She came closer and settled herself beside him. "Do you know not the proper etiquette in your country for the stickiness of dates?"

Escher shook his head, mutely. He was sweating. What did she want from him?

Hesperia reached for his hand and raised it slowly to her lips. With the tip of her tongue, she daintily licked each finger, then inserted the index finger in her mouth and sucked gently on it. Escher shivered.

Hesperia reached behind her and selected another date, conveyed this to her mouth. She nibbled this in a way that made him blush. Then she pressed her sticky fingers to his mouth. He bowed to the inevitable and kissed her fingertips.

This wasn't about sex or desire, he realized. This was a power play. Submit, or you'll end up as a door knocker, said the front door. Beware of demons in the bedchambers, said the paintings. But he hadn't conquered Hesperia's Rubik's Cube challenge by submitting; he had conquered it by facing it head on. The persona he was using wasn't up to this; he needed to modify it. A little bit of Kirk, a little bit of Bond ...

"I can tell there is something you want," she breathed. "You can hardly keep your eyes off it. You want my ..."

Involuntarily, his eyes flickered to her body, like a candle flame next to his own, then back to her face.

"You naughty mage. I was going to say you want my ruby."

"Must we speak in euphemisms?"

She laughed again, bells on a distant hillside.

"Gallant misdirection. You are a natural for the Game. Carry me to my chamber, and we will discuss — at length — what we might exchange."

She wrapped her arms around his neck, and he did this thing that he was bid.

Much later, Escher opened his eyes in a tangle of sheets. Hesperia lay across him where she had spent herself — she had predictably liked being on top. His alter ego had taken full advantage of the situation and now felt smugly satisfied. His inner self felt used, stained, tawdry. This was a stain that might never wash out or be entirely covered up. He was also disturbed that he felt such a vast disconnect with his alter ego. Was it possible that he truly was like that? How could he be both people?

Beyond the bed, he could see a large framed painting on the wall. He assumed it was a painting because this world had not yet invented photography. However, it was exceedingly, disturbingly realistic. It depicted a demonic creature, red and black, with flames licking over its body. It embraced a human woman in its arms; from the relative sizes, the demon must have been eight or nine feet tall. The woman seemed to welcome the embrace, even though her hair was smoldering, with one side already catching fire. There was an angry red handprint on one shoulder where the demon's hand had rested before shifting to her arm. Yet her face was tilted up, eyes closed, in apparent rapture. Escher found the entire composition profoundly disturbing, and in this his alter ego agreed.

He shifted slightly, but Hesperia slept on. His alter ego felt the twin pillows of her breasts flattened against his chest, but he knew the real prize was the ruby that hung pressed between them. Moving slowly and steadily, he began to roll to one side to extract himself from the tangle. He put one hand on her neck to cushion her head from flopping as he turned, while two fingers deftly undid the clasp on the chain of her pendant. Now she was cradled on her side and he was free to slide out of the bed. This was the moment of truth. Until now, he was easing out of the bed, and the ruby was plausibly knocked loose in their struggles. Escher checked her carefully once more; she appeared to still be deeply asleep, breathing steadily, eyes closed. He grasped the ruby in his hand and slid noiselessly from the bed. Now it was theft. He looked back as he was leaving; what he saw leant terror to his flight.

He quickly gathered his clothes and passed through the chamber door with no more sound than snowflakes falling on a still morning. He dressed and began searching for a way out. There were indeed many doors to the castle; he peered out one after another, searching for the one he needed. From some, he could see places where she could readily procure as many dates as she wished, though he would be glad not to see another one for a very long time. From others, he could have departed to places that were useful, and to not a few places that were disturbing. This castle seemed to open onto many different geogons; he wondered how she managed it. The amount of geomantic power she possessed to accomplish this added urgency to his search.

At last, he came to the one that he sought. He stepped out again onto a snowy scene, though one tamer and more pastoral than his entrance, and from which he could see Plurs in the distance. The snow and the hills dissolved as he took that step, and he found himself back in the hallway of the baker from which he had departed. He turned to look back and saw a small globe displayed on a shelf. Within the globe was a castle on a hillside, and snowflakes drifted and swirled around the castle in the liquid that filled the globe. He suppressed an urge to give the globe a good shake to stir up the storms again. The globe faded from sight before the urge had a chance of winning out.

No one was about. He opened the door onto the rooftop garden again, this time looking before he stepped through. The doorway did not abduct him on this occasion; he walked to the edge to see if there were any activity at his residence.

"Where have you been?"

"Trefoil! I'm glad you waited for me. Or did you go and come back?"

"When have I had time to leave? You were ahead of me going through the door, then you were nowhere to be seen, then you came through the door behind me. That's quite a trick."

"Just now? I feel like I was gone an entire day."

"Where did you go between one side of the door and the other?"

"I was visiting the Contessa Hesperia in her castle." His heart still pounded as he recalled his escape.

"Oh my, how did you get there?"

"She opened a door for me, invited me to solve her maze, entertained me in her parlor, and then … never mind."

"What did you do?"

"I stole her ruby."

"Oh, my. She's going to be angry."

"You have no idea." He couldn't bring himself to voice what he had seen in that bedchamber. The raven hair, now stringy and dirty white. The smooth golden skin, now gnarled like old mahogany. The toothless mouth like a wound in a nest of wrinkles. The ruby had been the agency keeping Hesperia young. Disturbing as all that was, the detail that his mind kept circling in horror was the old white scar on one shoulder, in the shape of a hand.

Clockmaker

The Plurs Chasm

Morning Edition, July 4, 2017

A man was found wandering in confusion near the Square of the Jewelers on the morning following the recent geomantic alignment. While many people experience minor disorientation after such an event, this seems to be an extreme case. The man wore foreign clothes and had unfamiliar currency in his pocket as if he had recently been traveling. He was unable or unwilling to give his name to authorities. He was lodged with a local charity overnight in the hopes that he would regain a sense of who he was, but he wandered away during the hours of darkness. He is described as of middle height and of athletic build with dark hair but is otherwise undistinguished in appearance.

The cat and the thief who called himself Escher went down to the street. "I have seen no activity over there since we arrived," said Trefoil. "I don't think Molendinarii has been there."

Escher studied the small house carefully. "No one has entered by doors or windows, at least."

"How can you tell?"

"Perspective alarms. They would look subtly wrong if someone other than us went through them."

"I'll go in first." Trefoil set off across the road, following his usual routine. He trotted to the other side, sniffed around the door of the seamstress's shop, leapt to the top of the flower box to see if he could glimpse the Angora that lived there, then down again. He stopped by the banker's door. His tail vibrated.

"Trefoil, do you have to mark his door every time?" muttered Escher. "He only throws shoes at you. He raises *my* interest rates."

The cat continued into the yard of their little house, stopped to stalk a bird that mocked him before flying away, peered into a hole in one corner that he suspected of admitting mice to the pantry, scaled a small flowering tree, and leapt from one of its branches to the windowsill. It was a perfect imitation of an unconcerned cat returning home. Trefoil disappeared inside, then reappeared a moment later in the signal that all was clear.

Escher crossed the street as well and quickly let himself in the front door. All was as he had left it. He studied the pattern of tiles on the mantlepiece once more. Each tile was from a scene in Escher's home in a different time and place and called for a response known only to him. It would be impossible for anyone other than him to respond with the correct code. He placed the ruby in the space that was revealed, then looked around for other items he would not want falling into the wrong hands, paws, or talons.

Next, he gathered up a small pile of books and placed them behind the tile, moving other books around to obscure that any were missing. He added a scroll depicting several impossible geometric figures and a woodblock print of a Japanese temple. These slid easily into the space despite it appearing to be only a few inches deep.

"I didn't know you had installed a non-Euclidean space in there," observed Trefoil. "Is it safe?"

"It's a bounded Riemann space. It should stay contained where I've confined it."

"And it won't distort any of the figures that you place in it, including three-dimensional projections of higher-order objects like that ruby?"

An expression of disquiet crossed Escher's face. "Well, it hasn't blown up yet. There must not have been any singularities in the mapping function."

"I honestly don't know how you've survived this long."

"What kind of cat did you say you were?"

"An alley cat. Just a common mogger."

"Where did you learn all this math?"

"It was a quite peculiar alley."

"I'd say. We need to find our own alley to hide out in now. I have to decide on my next move."

"You need something more defensible than an alley."

Escher dumped some colored stones on the table and began pushing them into patterns. This was a thing that he did when he needed to distract his math brain. That side of his brain was good for tactical thinking, but he needed to be more strategic. Trefoil began washing the street dust off his paws, then moved on to his face and ears when Escher continued to think.

"You're right, Trefoil."

"I am? Er, of course I am, but which part were you thinking of?"

"I need to start taking the initiative in this Game. If I keep letting these Players make the moves, I'll only get what they want, not what I want."

"Now you're thinking like a cat. To start with, if you play with the big kids, you will need your own castle. Something you can defend. This little cottage in the middle of town isn't suitable."

"I can't afford a castle."

"Perhaps the banker …"

"You've marked his door too many times."

"I can't help it if he happens to live in the house owned by that obnoxious orange pretender. I can accommodate black cats and white cats and tigers, but ginger toms are the worst."

"Focus, Trefoil."

"Oh. Right. Castle …"

Escher snapped his fingers. "I'll take over Moonbird's observatory. I'm starting to think she might have been a Player as well, which means she might have her own Knot storing geomantic power there. Even if she doesn't … didn't, it's still much more defensible than here."

"You were in a mighty hurry to get out of there. Now you want to go back?"

"I admit, I panicked. Now that I have time to think about it, the killer isn't very likely to go back there. He's taken his revenge, and won't expect to find me there. He's much more likely to look for me here, though I don't think there's a trail that would connect me to her anyway."

"Strong walls don't help if the door can be broken in."

"Doors can be reinforced. I'll tell people she was called away and asked me to be the caretaker in her absence. Now, what to do with the body?"

"I'm a cat. I would leave it on someone's doorstep."

"I'd love to leave it on Molendinarii's doorstep, but if I'm occupying her observatory, I think it will raise questions."

"You'll have to bury it yourself, then."

"I don't relish that task."

"It's too big for me. Is there anyone you trust to do it."

Escher sighed. "No, I'll have to do it, even though that will look even more suspicious if I'm caught. At my trial, I shall say that I took moral advice from a cat, and they will laugh as they hang me. However, I can't dispute your argument. Let us be off before someone else discovers the body."

❖

Late that afternoon, Escher climbed stiffly to his feet. He surveyed the bed of roses that he had planted (red roses, of course) and tried to convince himself that it did not look like a grave to eyes other than his own. He was glad that the observatory was perched on a tor high over the neighboring houses, so he had been able to do his gardening unobserved. He wondered if he should say something over the grave, but found that his feelings were conflicted. She had been kind, and she had given him the lead that he wanted but had failed to warn him how dangerous his opponent would be. She had given him that opaque warning about revenge, which he had no intention of heeding, without telling him what she knew or how she knew it. She hadn't been the sweet but slightly dotty old woman that she had seemed. Or not only that. After a few minutes of thought, Escher said only, "She made good tea."

Now, however, a small bell chimed silver in the air. Someone was ascending the path. "Trefoil, can you see who is coming? Friend or foe?"

Trefoil had been standing watch on the branch of a tree that had a strategic view of the upwards path. Standing might have been an exaggeration, for he was tightly curled on the branch, which also strategically caught the afternoon sun. Escher could swear that his eyes were closed, but he immediately reported, "It's no one I know. It's a short, fat man, carrying a case of tools. At this rate, it's going to take him a while to get to the top."

"I'll just have to send him away." Escher continued to putter about much more mundane bits of gardening than burying bodies under rose beds while inwardly rehearsing the impending encounter. Recent answers to the question "how badly could it go?" were not reassuring. After several long minutes, a florid man in a waistcoat came puffing up the walk. He stopped to catch his breath at the top, then approached the observatory. Escher moved to place himself in the man's path. The man hesitated, obviously wondering why a man that he perceived as a mere gardener would accost him.

"Lady Moonbird is not at home right now. Can I help you?"

The man scowled. "She's expecting me," he said shortly and made to step around Escher.

Escher moved to again block his path. "I'm sorry, she really isn't here right now. Can I tell her who has called on her when she returns?"

The visitor puffed out oversized white mustaches that emphasized the expanses of red cheek around them. "But I only saw her two days ago when she made an appointment for me to adjust her clockworks," he said somewhat suspiciously. "Why would she make an appointment if she knew she was going away?"

"She only just found out herself. I'm no expert in her field, but she gave me to understand that she had seen some remarkable alignment in the stars, just last night, that meant that she had to leave immediately. She asked me to take care of this place in her absence. But she did leave me some instructions, and there might be something about clocks among them. What was your name?"

"M. Fourquereau, clockmaker. I have taken care of her mechanisms for many years."

Escher decided that this intruder would best be mollified by allowing him to do his job. "Ah, yes. Now I recall. She did say you were coming and told me that you were to make your adjustments so that everything would run smoothly in her absence."

"And what is your name, sir?"

"M. Resche. I have a small business as a Scryer in town, on Twopenny Lane."

"Ah. I believe I have heard of you." Escher had debated giving his business name or one of his many aliases and decided that it would be more plausible if Moonbird had asked an established community member to watch her place. As Fourquereau's face relaxed, Escher felt relieved that it seemed to have been the right choice.

Fourquereau allowed Escher to conduct him to the upper floors. Escher had, as his first item of business, disarmed the perspective trap on the stairs. Now, he watched in interest as Fourquereau opened panels that he had only guessed at, inspected the gear bearings and teeth, and applied small amounts of lubricant to the ends of several rods. He stopped and sniffed, then ran his finger around a bearing and inspected the tip. "This bearing smells burned. The metal is discolored as if it has been heated, and there are flakes of brass in the bearing cup. That is most unusual for a clock mechanism."

Fourquereau started to wind the counterweight and stopped in surprise. "It's wound all the way down," he said. He examined the governor, then turned to Escher. "Who has damaged this magnificent mechanism?" His mustaches trembled with suppressed rage.

"What? Show me!" Escher feigned outrage. In truth, he had forgotten that he had broken the mechanism in his escape from the tower, with his intervening stay in Hesperia's castle. He began to second-guess his decision to let the clockmaker in.

"See, these arms are broken. I shall have to cast new ones. This is a unique movement for which there are no replacement parts. Who could have committed this vandalism?" He looked pointedly at Escher.

"I couldn't say. Lady Moonbird was quite insistent in her instructions that nobody be permitted to make observations here for the next seven days. Perhaps she did not want anyone else to discover whatever she saw last night?"

Fourquereau inspected the governor once more. "I have a hard time crediting that. Surely she could have found a less expensive way to prevent the use of her equipment."

"Please do make replacements for the broken pieces. I'll have payment arranged for whatever you think to be a fair price for the work. The Lady has given me full authority for the upkeep of the place."

"It won't be cheap. I shall have to replace several of the brass bearings as well. They are deformed enough that they will provide uneven movement for now, and will eventually seize."

"As you think best."

Fourquereau made extensive notes on the parts that he would need then packed his tools to leave. As they descended the stairs, Escher was just beginning to let himself think that he had successfully diverted Fourquereau's suspicions when the clockmaker stopped abruptly on the forty-second stair. He narrowed his eyes as he looked up, then down, the stairs, and ran his hand over the wall. Escher's heart was pounding as he tried to keep the expression out of his face by counting the stones in the wall. After a moment, Fourquereau shook his head and said, "Thought I felt a draft," and continued down-ward.

Escher's inaudible sigh of relief was premature. Four-quereau stopped at the exterior door and peered closely at the lock, and then back up the stairs. "This lock has been broken from the inside," he said. "Did you know that?"

"From inside?" Esher didn't need to feign surprise; he hadn't had time to repair the lock and hadn't looked closely at it.

"Do you see? The bar is broken where the door was forced inwards, but the handle on the inside is bent from the force, not the one on the outside."

Fourquereau puffed into his mustaches, considering. He shot Escher a sharp glance before saying, "This doesn't look good. She may have told you that she was going away because of an Astromantic portent, but I believe she may have been fleeing for her life. She came to me several weeks ago with a prediction made by some priest that a new geomantic alignment was pending, and that dangerous people were going to use it to upset the balance of power. Step lightly, because it appears that she may have angered people with a great deal to gain and few scruples about how they do so."

Second Scrying

The Plurs Chasm

October 12, 2017

The Town Tax Office wishes to remind residents that the brick tax is due on the 30th of November, and the window tax is due by the 30th of March. Owners with new construction, or who have alterations affecting either of these measures, should schedule an audit by the Town no less than thirty days before the taxes are due. We should also remind property owners of their responsibility to maintain at least one lamp illuminated on the street before their building at all times between the hours of sunset and sunrise. Residents situated at an intersection can post a single lamp on the corner of their building if they so choose.

The sun was sinking into low clouds near the horizon, spelling an approaching end to daylight, when the bell on the path rang once more. The man named Escher went to the window to look down. "This is when Lady Moonbird schedules her clients, isn't it? I suppose I'll have to go down and tell them there will be no astromancy performed for some time. I don't expect it will make any material difference in the world."

He descended the stairs and took the bench seat underneath the tree that bore the wind chimes. They shed no notes in the quiet air this evening, and the birds were also taking their rest. Trefoil came to sit beside him while he waited. After several minutes a slender figure crested the hill and walked purposefully towards them. This person didn't appear at all winded by the ascent. The sun was behind her — for the silhouette was definitely feminine — and while he couldn't make out any features, Escher began to think he had seen this stride before.

However, he was clearly lit by the setting sun, and evidently recognizable. The figure stopped and said, "You!" in a voice that he immediately identified as Emeline Cigne's.

"Uh-oh."

He stood, about to offer an apology, but she cut him off. "When someone makes an appointment with me and fails to send as much as a note of regret after I have put off important people and asked someone else to write my column for today, I at least expect to find them occupying a hospital bed, if not a berth in the morgue. Yet here you are, apparently the picture of good health. What could possibly explain this lapse?"

"My apologies, Mademoiselle. I was called here late last night by my associate, Lady Moonbird, who had to leave abruptly on an extended trip. She asked me to take care of her place in her absence and to give her regrets to any clients that she had been unable to contact. As for our own appointment … to my great shame, I simply forgot about it in the whirlwind of the day. However, now that you're here, this is probably an even better location to perform your second scrying."

Emeline stood for a moment, weighing his words. A late breeze stole over the hilltop as the sun dropped below the cloud tops, moving the dark tresses that fell about her shoulders and eliciting soft comments from the wind chimes. She gave a sigh and nodded. "Let us do that. I still want to locate my compass, and you're telling me I cannot have the session with Lady Moonbird that I scheduled, so we seem to have both the time and the place for doing this."

Escher gestured for her to proceed him into the observatory and up the stairs. This placed him eye level with her practical boots and the edge of her ankle-length skirt, which she held knotted in one hand to ascend the steps while she kept the other hand on the stone wall. The stairs had no railing or barrier between them and a short trip to the bottom, so caution was warranted. Trefoil waited until they were a dozen steps up, then zoomed past their feet and disappeared ahead of them. A moment later, his small face with the white blaze looked over the side of a higher flight, waiting for them to catch up. This drew a tiny chuckle from Emeline.

At the top of the stairs, Escher took her cloak and hung it on a peg, and invited her to sit on the couch. He had a moment of panic remembering that Lady Moonbird's body had lain there only that morning, which he concealed by turning to the small kitchen nook to look for vessels that he could use for scrying. He soon returned with a plain white porcelain bowl, a large cup, and a pitcher of water. He found some lengths of cord as well that he could use for the Knots. Soon fog streamed across the floor. Fortunately, instruments to measure angles were plentiful in the observatory, and the cardinal directions were inscribed on the dome. He made careful note of the azimuth, and then rechecked his measurement. He turned to Emeline, glad that they had gotten that fix, and both relieved and disappointed that no vision had appeared in the bowl. But now the fog was lit from within by a candle. The candle receded slowly from them, and its light fell upon the compass and the hand that held it. As it continued to withdraw from them, a head came into view, covered in a nimbus of white hair, bent to the study of the compass. Escher strained to see who it might be, but eddying breezes shredded the fog, carrying wisps of identity off into the room to evaporate and vanish.

These visions were something new. Escher pondered what might have changed. He had only learned of his talent for scrying six months ago; was it possible that he had simply become more skillful? Or was there something different about either this client or the thing she desired? The first of these made him wary, and the second drew his interest.

"It appears that whoever owns it suspects what they have," commented Emeline.

"And just what do they have?" inquired Escher.

"A compass, of course." There was an air of both whimsy and challenge to her statement.

"I didn't bring the map with me. In the morning, I can plot this line on the map at my shop. Can you come there again tomorrow? I promise that nothing will prevent me from keeping the appointment this time."

Emeline weighed him with her eyes. The lamplight fell on the right side of her face, throwing shadows on her left that accented her cheekbones. Escher had thought her oval face was somewhat plain, but in this light he could see that her mouth was a little more generous and her brow a little broader than a classic oval shape. It was the way her hair framed her face that had made it seem narrow. But now a slight amusement visited her eyes and drew up the corners of her mouth, which brightened even the dim lamplight. He wanted to study her face a little longer, but he looked down because that's what normal people did. People who didn't have to study other people to memorize what they should do in situations like this.

"I have commitments until early afternoon, and it would be better to meet at the newspaper office, as we planned today. Shall we say the second hour of the afternoon?"

"That will be fine. I will be certain to be there."

Emeline rose and donned her cloak. "I'm sure you will be. No one has ever missed an appointment with me a second time." It was much softer than a threat because of the smile that accompanied it. But it was definitely a promise.

❖

"I wonder what other guests we'll have dropping in on us?" said Trefoil.

"That's an excellent question. I hope Lady Moonbird was organized enough to keep an appointment book." Escher ventured into the cyclonic cubbyhole that seemed to have served as an office. A desk was piled high with astronomical charts, books, old papers, and other assorted paraphernalia. He started by trying to scan the materials on the top layer, on the theory that something as often-used as an appointment book would be near the top. But his mind wouldn't allow that approach. There were six hundred and fifty-seven pieces of paper visible on the desk and seventeen bound volumes. There were forecasts and bills and grocery orders ... He grimaced and started sorting the paper into piles that he could make sense of.

The oil lamp was guttering low by the time he finished, forcing him to find oil to refill it before continuing. Appointments had been written on scraps of paper, margins of ledgers, and backs of envelopes. She had been booked most evenings, sometimes with two or three clients. Emeline had indeed had an appointment this evening, and he found his own appointment from two weeks ago, under his assumed name. However, Lady Moonbird had had no appointment yesterday evening; Molendinarii had not had the courtesy to schedule his assassination. Strangely, there were no appointments after today.

"Did she know that she was 'going away' last night?" he asked Trefoil. The cat was tucked into a neat package resembling a loaf of bread, eyes tightly shut. He made only a low huffing sound. "But if she could foretell that," Escher continued, "why would she need appointments? She could just forecast which clients would come each evening." Trefoil yawned.

One stack in front of Escher was issues of the *Plurs Chasm*, the local newspaper. It was a six-column Berliner-format paper with a sober tone. Escher sorted them into chronological sequence, not because he was trying to learn anything from them but because he simply couldn't move on to the next task until he had imposed a satisfactory order on them. One issue, thirty-two days ago, caught his eye. An article on the front page had been marked up and a name circled. A priest named Wharnebie was issuing a prediction of another geomantic realignment within the next two months. The article explained that these were widely believed to be continued settling from the original Geography Disaster, four hundred years in the past. At intervals ranging from a decade to nearly a century, the geogons of the earth shifted slightly, much the way the ground slipped along a fault line during an earthquake. Sometimes you ended up with new neighbors entirely. Most of the others interviewed discounted the warning. The previous realignment had been a mere ten months ago, and only once in history had two realignments occurred that closely together. The mayor appealed to the city not to panic.

This had to be the same priest that Fourquereau had mentioned. Escher decided that he had time in the morning to seek out this priest before he met with Emeline. He might be able to find out more about how the Game used the realignments. Then he noticed that the byline on the article was Emeline

Cigne. He wondered why she was writing stories if she was owner and publisher. The next several issues of the newspaper answered his question as he found a series of reports by Emeline on how business leaders and politicians profited from the current alignment and would go to great lengths to prevent a run on markets that might be affected by a new alignment, when new trading partners might suddenly share a border with Plurs. It seemed that Emeline was a muckraker, in a world where the term had never been invented.

Searching for a Priest

The Plurs Chasm

August 17, 1903 (from the archives)

Detective Peabody of the Plurs constabulary has cracked the long string of forged drafts, deeds, and other financial instruments that have threatened to undermine commerce in our town. The crimes have been marked by financial documents that have been stamped and signed in imitations of the victims' own handwriting so convincing that in many cases the person themselves could not distinguish a real sample of their signature from the forged one. Beyond the financial losses, there have been a string of embarrassed and discommoded individuals, many highly-placed, who have had to deny what appeared to be clear proof that they had entered into questionable transactions.

Detective Peabody yesterday arrested Mabel Preece, age 25, who was also known as Cecilia Singerly and Mabel Price, with ages of 22 and 27, respectively. Her landlady grew suspicious of the burning of a large number of documents in the small hours of the morning, and upon searching the premises, Detective Peabody found numerous unexecuted documents along with samples of the handwriting of people who had been defrauded. The young lady, who is as calm as you please in the face of the accusations, is in jail awaiting her appointment with the Magistrates later this week.

The next day, the man who sometimes called himself Resche went to find the priest.

"Priests have temples, or sometimes cathedrals. I haven't seen either in town. Or churches. Or even chapels. Where do you keep priests if you don't have the right container for them? They tend to spoil if they're just left out on the streets."

"What was his name, again?" inquired Trefoil as he slicked back a whisker with a paw.

"Wharnebie."

"I don't know that name. Of course, to be a big name among cats, you either need to be generous with the table scraps or known for throwing boots."

"I see. I don't suppose there are any hermit priests around?"

"None known to cats."

"Understandable that hermits wouldn't have much food to share, and probably don't have any boots to throw either."

"Yeah, that makes them pretty much invisible to cats."

"Say … I know who has a list of everyone in town!"

An hour later, a smoky grey cat slipped from an alleyway leading onto the town square and crossed to the fountain in the center. The pigeons wisely left before he arrived. The cat put his paws on the edge and looked within, just in case there were any goldfish within reach. There never had been, but the cat knew that didn't mean there never would be. He sat down and began to wash his face.

Escher watched from the same dim alleyway. When he was satisfied that no one was watching, he lowered the hood of his cloak. Figures in dark alleys wore concealing hoods, but not those crossing open plazas. It was a cliché, but clichés were useful. People saw what they expected to see. He shook out a simple Knot and held it in his hand as he entered the plaza with an unhurried air. The Knot didn't make him invisible; it made him uninteresting. As long as he didn't call attention to himself, none would remember his passage.

Escher entered the building across the square to the left of Town Hall. It was low, unimaginative and frugal in design, and possessed a very strongly fortified room in the rear. The sign over the doorway proclaimed this to be the office of the town tax collector.

Within was a scene of organized clutter. Shelves were laden with roll books that recorded taxes assessed and paid. One wall was covered with hundreds of cubbyholes, most stuffed to overflowing with scrolls, certificates, and maps. The entirety was presided over from a seat at a towering roll-top desk by a matron of imposing rotundity, who could maintain a cheery and motherly demeanor while emptying your pockets of every penny they contained, plus the lint.

"Good day, Mrs. Hazard," he said, remembering that she preferred the English honorific to the French.

"Well, Master Resche! How nice to see you. What brings you here today? You've already paid the lamplighter tax, and the brick and window tax isn't due until the end of the month."

He had a gambit ready to get the information he wanted without raising suspicions. He was probably being more devious than this situation required, but old habits and all that. "Yes, well, I was wondering if you would explain how that works. I was new in town last year, and there seemed to be an endless train of taxes and fees when I acquired my modest shop. I just paid everything that was asked to get myself set up. But this brick and window tax is unfamiliar to me, and I'd like to understand it."

"Oh, it's simple enough, Master Reche. We charge 12 pence per window per year, and 8 pence per thousand bricks on your exterior. It's such a nice way to do it. We can count everything from the outside without disturbing you, and everyone can see that it's fair and accurate. And if people build out of wood or stone, we just use the equivalent in square footage to figure out how many bricks they would have if they had used bricks."

"I see. There's one window that's exclusively used by my cat as a means of egress. I wonder if I could get it reclassified as a door?"

"Oh, you're so funny, Master Reche!"

"So everyone pays the same rates? Even churches and schools?"

"We even pay ourselves a tax every year for the bricks and windows in this building! We do love recursion in this town."

"Interesting. Where I come from, churches are exempt from taxes."

"Well, that sets a pretty poor example, doesn't it?"

"Since they aren't exempt here, might you know where a priest named Wharnebie plies his calling? I have an envelope that was left with me by mistake. It has only his name on it."

Mrs. Hazard's face darkened. "The Fractalists!"

"Is there something wrong, Mrs. Hazard?"

"After all we've done to create a fair and equitable system, without loopholes and exceptions, they had to come along and throw a singularity into it. The perimeter of their building cannot be measured, Master Resche! We can't agree on the tax to charge them. Meanwhile, they get away without paying the brick tax, and others begin to get the idea that they can figure out their own dodge. That's how civilizations begin to collapse, sir! They start to make exceptions to the rules."

"I presume their building has a fractal perimeter then? I see. Might I suggest scribing the smallest circle around their building that contains their perimeter and using that for the area? It will be slightly larger than a conventional building built on that lot, but a great deal smaller than infinity. They may find that an acceptable compromise. If you could tell me their address, I can drop off this letter, and while I'm there, I could look at their exterior. I enjoy mathematics and I might be able to make a recommendation to you."

A slow smile came over Mrs. Hazard. "That might just work. That's very civic-minded of you, Master Resche. If I find it acceptable, I'm sure they can be *convinced* to accept it as well." She wrote it out on a slip of paper and passed it to him.

Escher shivered slightly at the bureaucratic malice behind that smile. "Glad to be of service. Perhaps I could deduct a small consulting fee from my next tax bill?"

"Don't push your luck, Master Resche."

Escher and Trefoil made their way to the address that Mrs. Hazard had given them. "I fail to understand how that solution hadn't occurred to them," said Trefoil.

"Do you recall seeing a shred of imagination or creativity in that office?" said Escher.

"I can't say that I did."

"They were told to count bricks, so count bricks they must. It was an almost inconceivable leap for them to use imaginary bricks to calculate the tax on a wooden house. Introducing a virtual surface to hold the imaginary bricks was beyond them. Still, this will bend the rule just enough. People will get ideas. Other exceptions will be found. The eventual collapse of civilization will be traced to this day."

"You're as sarcastic as an old tomcat."

"I'll take that as a compliment," said Escher.

Two streets later, they turned a corner. "This seems to be the place … Oh my!"

The building was in the shape of a Koch snowflake. It started with three sides, but then each side was divided into three segments and bumped out to become a hexagram. Then each segment was again divided into three, and the process was repeated recursively until the edge was a lacy frill of ridges down to the limits of visual perception. If it were a true Koch snowflake, the perimeter would be infinitely long, enclosing a finite area. Escher could appreciate that it would drive the literal Mrs. Hazard batty.

The entrance was through a set of stairs that led down below ground level then back up within the structure, so the fractal nature of the walls was not pierced by something as mundane as a doorway.

He emerged into a candlelit interior. The ceiling rose in a dome that seemed higher than it should be from the outside of the building. Escher thought that it could be an illusion that the indirect lighting cast on a painting of a lightly clouded sky. At least, he thought it was a painting. He stood in a narrow channel of walls that were just high enough to prevent him from seeing over. He lifted Trefoil to the top of the wall, where he reported that it looked like he was in a deeply folded maze. The walls of the maze were inscribed with many different fractal designs. Escher identified Mandelbrot sets, Julia sets, Sierpinski Triangles, and depictions of natural fractals such as spiral shells and branching trees. At regular intervals was a reproduction of the Koch snowflake, leading the viewer to think of one figure with an infinite boundary held inside a building with a likewise infinite boundary.

Escher motioned Trefoil to stay atop the wall to help navigate. He made his way through several turnings of the passage, until he came upon a young woman in the simple robes of a novice, laboriously drawing another figure upon the wall.

"Your pardon, but I'm looking for a priest named Wharnebie," he addressed her.

With an unhurried manner, she laid down her brush and stepped over to inspect the nearest Koch snowflake on the wall. "He is very far away right now, but if you continue in this passage and take the first two left turns, then a right, then two more lefts, you should find him."

Escher continued as instructed, while Trefoil slipped past the novice, unseen.

Fractalism

𝕿𝖍𝖊 𝕻𝖑𝖚𝖗𝖘 𝕮𝖍𝖆𝖘𝖒

April 23, 2012

The Plurs Museum is proud to announce the acquisition of a Roman chariot that was unearthed two years ago and which has been painstakingly restored to nearly its original condition. Dating from the first century, it appears to have been buried for unknown reasons, and recently revealed by a slippage of earth. Historians are trying to determine how the chariot came to be located here, although there is a strong possibility that geomantic realignments have carried it far from the location where it was originally situated. One scholar lamented the degree to which the Geography Disaster set back the field of archaeology by re-ordering the layers in which these old artifacts lay in the ground.

The man who called himself Escher walked through the maze, paced by the smoke-colored cat. He made note of each turn they made while Trefoil fretted. "What if we get lost in here?"

"We can always employ Trémaux's algorithm to eventually find our way out, though it might take years in a maze of this size."

"I'll starve!"

"Is that the first thing you think about?"

"Let's see. Food, sleep, sex, things to chase. Yep, that's about the top of the list. Second place is a toss-up."

"There must be a principle for finding your way through this place, otherwise they'd be misplacing supplicants at every turn. It's fairly obviously a multicursal maze since we traversed branches. We don't know if it's looping or simply-connected; we have to assume looping unless we find out otherwise. I'm going to assume that the solution relies on the application of a principle rather than memorization because that seems to be the mindset of these people. Where does that leave us?"

"Still in a maze," said Trefoil gloomily.

They came at last to a doorway. Escher passed through the doorway into a large chamber while Trefoil lurked just outside. A figure in a brown robe stood contemplating an intricate fractal mandala that filled most of the floor. He was hunched over with a spine that hadn't grown straight, head cocked to one side in a permanent bird-like attitude. A tall walking stick grasped in both hands completed the tripod that kept him upright.

"Pardon me, I am looking for a Priest named Wharnebie."

"I am Wharnebie, yes," came the reply. The voice was both stronger and higher-pitched than Escher had expected. He had an unplaceable accent. The Priest said nothing more, waiting patiently for the next question, or for nothing at all.

"I believe that it might be to our mutual interest to talk," ventured Escher.

"Do you wish to talk about the nature of infinity? It is my main concern, that."

Escher smiled a one-sided smile. "I fear that conversation would never end."

Wharnebie fixed Escher with a single eye. The other one, having business of its own, wandered off to the right. "Young man, you clearly need to know your limits, yes."

"I tend to shun integrals," he replied. Trefoil found the urgent need to groom his left shoulder, the cat equivalent of a groan.

Wharnebie looked closely at Escher. "Yes, you would, wouldn't you?"

Escher looked aside, uncomfortable. His eyes fell on the mandala in the floor, which he felt an immediate compulsion to trace to its end. "So. A man with a crooked back, in a maze, with a design on the floor. If you walk the design to its center, can you step from there to anywhere that you can hold in your mind?"

Wharnebie frowned. "No. Why would you think that?"

"Of course not. Wrong story. Please excuse me."

"Then why is it you wish to speak to me?"

"I recently read the newspaper article in which you warned of an impending geomantic realignment. I've read as much as I could find about these realignments since I arrived here a year ago, but you're the first person I've heard who claims to be able to predict them. I want to learn what you know about them."

"I see. What is your interest in these events? I think it is not merely academic, no."

Escher hesitated, but could see no reason for keeping this part a secret. "I arrived here — unexpectedly — during the last event. I have been unable to find my way back to the city I lived in prior to that day. I have business of considerable personal importance that I left unfinished, so I very much want to get back."

Wharnebie considered this. "I was not aware that any of the boundaries of Plurs were changed by that event, that day. Even if they were, the configurations have been stable since then, yes. You should be able to retrace your steps, at least up until the time that the next realignment occurs. Then, anything can happen. Though neighboring geogons seldom move more than one hop away, yes."

"That's the thing. That city doesn't exist in this world. And my world isn't broken up into scrambled and shifting geogons as this one is. I had never heard the term geomantic realignment until I walked out of a fog bank and heard everyone talking about it. It was like right after a small earthquake; everyone asks each other, 'Did you feel it?' "

The Priest walked to a bench near the wall and sat on one end. The word *walk* described his gait with the same accuracy as it did a crab's — that is to say, very little — involving much sidewise indirection of the feet and staccato punctuation with his walking stick. Escher took the emptiness of the bench's other end as an invitation and sat as well.

"I have speculated that there are other versions of this world, yes. Perhaps one in which the Disaster didn't happen, yes, in which lands were still arranged in their original and somewhat sensible order. Further, it might be possible for someone to fall through the cracks between the geogons, yes, and find themselves in a different world. Of course, there is no way to verify your story, as much as you may be convinced yourself of what you remember."

Escher started to protest then decided that the Priest was correct. "Fair point, but I don't want to write a dissertation on the dynamics of the multiverse. I simply want to return to my home."

"It may be difficult or impossible. Why do you want to return so badly? This is a prosperous town. You are dressed as if you have made a comfortable life for yourself here, yes. Is there someone you wish to see again?"

"You might say that." Escher tried to keep his voice level, but Wharnebie cocked an eye at the lack of warmth in this statement.

"I see. Someone has wronged you, no?"

"I ... I have a desire for justice. Let's leave it at that."

"As you wish. I am always here, and am sworn to keep confidences, should you ever feel moved to talk with someone."

"Er, thank you. I'm unused to that sort of offer."

"You should consider giving up this desire and becoming content with your life here, yes. You could become an initiate at the temple, and join us in our practice of Fractalism. You have the tracing eye; I can see the mandalas catching it every time you glance that direction, yes."

Escher felt the overwhelming attraction of tracing mandalas for the rest of his life and shuddered. "Just out of curiosity, what does your practice consist of?"

"We believe that the path to enlightenment is the contemplation of the infinite repetition of fractal forms, yes. In the contemplation of these forms are beauty and inner peace. We believe that if one studies these forms, one can develop within one's mind the perfect fractal, the one that corresponds with the deep structure of the Cosmos, and in doing so become one with it, yes."

"Has anyone ever attained this state?"

"Our founder did, yes, as have a small handful of his followers since then."

"Can they not just tell everyone else the shape of the perfect fractal?"

"Alas, no. After conceiving the Cosmic Fractal, they vanished from our world. In the last moments, as they approached the limits of perfection, they reported a transcendent bliss. While our individual goal is to reach that state ourselves, yes, the goal of our order is to eventually render the Cosmic Fractal visible so that all can partake of its transcendent nature."

"Would that be the end of the Cosmos, or only of humanity?"

"Neither! People would still live full and rewarding lives, yes, knowing that when they are ready to go beyond this world, they will come to a shrine such as this one and gaze upon the greatest and most final sight of their life."

Escher shivered. "What if they don't go to a place of bliss when they leave? How can you tell they don't just drop into another world, as I did?"

"We have mathematical proofs that say, in summary, that the entropic process of the Cosmic Fractal is the opposite of death, and is therefore one of greater life and awareness."

"I don't feel I'm cut out for a life of contemplation or for merging myself with the Cosmos; it makes it hard to do business. But these realignments ... can they be used? Manipulated?"

"There are some people who boast they can do this, yes. This is a very dangerous thing."

"I have encountered several people recently who have claimed they are players of some great Game. Are these the people you speak of?"

Wharnebie sprang up and erratically paced the length of the chamber. Escher eyed Wharnebie's walking stick and revised his assessment that the Priest was unarmed. The Priest whirled to fix Escher with both eyes. "Those fractional radicals are a blight on higher mathematics and enlightenment. There is no harmony in what they do, no. Their Game is entirely for their individual benefit, no matter the cost to anyone else. They hoard the geomantic energy released when geogons realign to build and reinforce their castles and their magical defenses. They seek to move geogons into configurations more advantageous to themselves or that undercut their opponents."

Escher weighed what he should reveal. "Did Lady Moonbird, the Astromancer, speak with you about these matters?"

"She did, yes. She grew concerned over the dangers, and was working to persuade some of the lesser Players to moderate or oppose their more radical members."

"She was a Player herself, then?"

"A minor one, primarily interested in the connection between geomantic alignments and astromantic projections. But what do you mean by saying she *was* a Player?"

Escher kicked himself for his slip. How much could he trust Wharnebie? "I believe she was threatened and departed for a place of safety. I am serving as caretaker of her observatory in her absence. I don't think she'll be a Player in this round."

"I see. What was your true purpose in seeking me out, then?" Escher could feel suspicion stirring in Wharnebie, all for the incautious choice of tense of a single verb.

"It is as I said, I am displaced from my home and wish to return. The Game may be responsible for my situation and is likely to be my way back. I have encountered Lord Molendinarii and Contessa Hesperia, and neither of them seemed inclined to help."

"Hesperia! Phagh! She is said to have the castle most extensive, though that also renders her more vulnerable to realignments that cut her off from portions of her empire. Lord Molendinarii is more subtle in the deployment of his power, trading reach for depth. These are the two most powerful Players, yes, though there are a number of minor ones who work in their shadows for their own gain."

"How do you come to know so much about the Game?"

"Fractalists wish to move the world back to its original configuration, yes. In this, we oppose the Players who seek states of greater chaos."

"Thus, you are a Player yourself." Escher was aware that he was baiting his informant and that it wasn't a good idea, but he couldn't help himself.

Wharnebie looked him over with his one steady eye as if trying to assess Escher's tendency towards dark arts. "No! I oppose this Game. The world is not a puzzle to be twisted and rearranged for the good of a few people."

"You would still rearrange the world, only your own assessment that the goal is a more worthy one separates you from them."

Wharnebie brought his wandering eye to bear on Escher, giving his steadier eye a head start towards the exit. This eye was distant, judging, already halfway to the place where the Cosmic Fractal lived. "The goal is what matters, yes. Think on this as you try to find your way out of the maze." With that he scuttled through a doorway faster than Escher would have credited. Escher was only two steps behind him, but the Priest was nowhere to be seen.

"We seem to be back to the starvation scenario," said Trefoil.

"I'm sure I can retrace our path," said Escher. "It might just take a while."

"Didn't you have an appointment with Emeline in the afternoon?"

"Oh, Dirac! That's in an hour. I have to hurry, and I still have to go by the shop to pick up the map." They walked through the maze until they got to the first intersection. It didn't seem familiar. "This was a left turn coming in, so it should be a right turn going out. But the angles seem wrong."

"Trust your memory, or at least trust my nose," said Trefoil. "It's a right."

"How … oh, you marked the wall." Escher could see the small yellow droplets six inches above the floor. "That's cheating."

"Hey, you're the one with the appointment."

"Under the circumstances, I'll take the assist."

They continued. The way out seemed longer than the way in, and the intersections had more branches than before. "We're at a higher level of fractal detail," said Escher. "Like when the Koch snowflake divides and subdivides its edges."

"It's a good thing that scent isn't fractal in nature," said Trefoil. "This way."

Even with Trefoil's nose, it took a large part of their hour to return to the entrance. Fractal edges approached infinity without enclosing any more area. Escher thought he had never seen a better demonstration of that principle, but he would gladly have deferred it to another time. Just inside the door, he stopped. There were voices outside, both familiar.

"… looking for a thief," Molendinarii was saying. "He entered my castle on a pretext, even had dinner at my table, then entered my vault and tried to steal something of great value. He gave his name as Escher, though I'm sure that was false." He put a snarl on the words "pretext" and "false." (But not "steal," thought Escher. Interesting.)

"I know no thieves," said Wharnebie. "Though I do know some politicians, yes. They don't make good fractalists. Fractalists need to see things as they are, not as they wish they were."

Molendinarii made an impatient sound at the irrelevance of this answer, but his reply was inaudible as if he had faced away from them. Wharnebie answered, "I will let you know, yes."

Escher and Trefoil waited for several minutes, then, hearing no further voices, hastened out into the streets. Escher glanced back. A shadow that might have been a crooked man with a walking stick watched from within as they departed.

Newspaper Office

The Plurs Chasm

March 11, 1976 (from the archives)

The Plurs police department has become aware of reports that a large strongbox of jewelry was stolen from the country estate of a prominent family, who do not wish to be identified. One night the strongbox was removed from the owner's room as she slept, but none of the windows or doors showed signs of entry. The family has engaged private parties to look into the theft, bypassing the police. Pawnbrokers report having been shown a list of gemstones for which they should be on the lookout, but none have been allowed to retain the list. One pawnbroker did recall that a particularly large ruby was among the stolen gems, lamenting that he would be unable to sell such a large piece in any event. In response to reports that one or more of the jewels have geomantic powers, the family has issued a denial through the offices of their solicitor, going so far as to say that the rumor that any gems have such powers was only folklore.

The chimes of the second hour of the afternoon had just rolled through the town in a sea of echoes and reflections when the man named Escher arrived at the offices of the *Plurs Chasm*. The building was of quarried stone with a regiment of windows tall and narrow facing the street. It had the air of the working-class cousin of a bank.

Escher entered the front door, at the top of well-worn concrete stairs. He was assaulted by the thump of the printing presses, and scents of paper and ink. There was no obvious receptionist, so Escher accosted the first harried person who crossed his path. "I have an appointment with Mademoiselle Cigne. Can you direct me to her?"

"Emeline!" He called over his shoulder. "You have a visitor."

Emeline came to the door of a nearby office. The plaque on the door said "Managing Editor," but someone had placed a neatly hand-written sign above it that read "Avenging Editor." She inclined her head as she stood aside to admit him. "M. Resche. I'm glad you remembered our appointment … this time." Trefoil ghosted in behind, apparently unnoticed.

The office was spacious but still managed to be cluttered. Beside the scarred mahogany desk that took up much of the center of the room, the walls were lined with mismatched tables that provided additional workspaces — or more often stacking spaces for piles that reached sedimentary densities at the bottom. Notes were piled in drifts, affixed to stacks, books, objects, and each other. On the wall, framed newspapers preserved moments that their subjects likely would prefer be forgotten: the fraud pinned on a local lender, the incumbent mayor who had lost his re-election, and more. The chaos was unsettling; the urge to square up the stacks and count their contents was almost irresistible.

Emeline's manner nettled Escher. She was the one who needed him to find the compass. He got to the point. "Here's the map we made last night. I haven't transferred the new measurement to it yet since I thought you might want to be present for that. Is there a place to lay it out?"

"Yes, I can make a clear space." She walked over to one of the side tables, and for a shuddering moment, Escher thought she would sweep all the piles off onto the floor and he would be forced to run screaming out the door. She pulled on a wire hanging near the wall, causing a wooden panel to hinge down, producing a fresh work surface on top of the existing piles. Escher thought about sedimentary papers being compressed into metamorphic strata under pressure, shale into slate. He told himself it was less chaotic that way.

"I had these made so I could spread out something new that comes in without disturbing work in progress on longer projects," she explained.

Escher gestured helplessly at the geologic piles of paper scattered around the room. "All of this is work in progress?"

"Some are long-term projects," she admitted.

"If they were any longer-term, plate tectonics would start moving them around." He realized as he spoke that he had inserted his internal metaphor into the conversation, and Emeline would wonder where that came from. That wasn't her question, though.

"Plate tectonics? Does that have anything to do with the plates we use for printing?"

"No, that's the term for the continents slowly drifting over the surface of the earth."

"That sounds rather fanciful. Where did you come up with that?"

Right. How could scientists have measured continental drift if the very continents had been divided into geogons and shuffled like a Mah Jong game? The movement of the geogons would hide the much smaller drift of the continents. "It's just a theory I heard, which I imagine is hard to prove." He didn't necessarily conceal that he came from a different world, but neither did he advertise it. Becoming known as delusional would be bad for business. But from some of the articles he had read, Emeline seemed to have an affinity for far-away lands and the explorers who sought them. She might not dismiss his story.

"I have heard stranger. My uncle Piers claims to have seen the bones of leviathans that once walked the earth. That would change much of what we know of natural history, if true."

"This is something I know to be true."

Emeline leaned forward at that. "Later, I would like to hear how you can say that with such assurance. For now, let's see if we can locate my uncle's compass."

Escher nodded and unrolled the map on the board. Emeline weighted the corners with a box of broken type, a bolt, and a doorstop. She was casting around for a fourth weight when Trefoil leapt on the table to sit primly on the final corner.

"You do turn up everywhere, don't you?" she said.

"He goes where he wishes," said Escher quickly.

"I imagine that he does, but I did him the courtesy of addressing him directly." She turned back to the cat. "And what is your name?"

Trefoil sat for the space of two slow blinks, then replied, "You could not pronounce my name, but he who buys whitefish for me calls me Trefoil. I suppose it suits."

"It does, with that handsome three-lobed marking that you wear on your forehead. I suppose your sooty footprint on the corner of the map lends it authenticity, but I must ask you not to walk on any of my other papers."

Trefoil waved his tail lazily in reply.

Escher pulled out the paper with the azimuth reading he had taken at the observatory. With a protractor, he carefully measured the angle from due north that corresponded to that direction. Of course, the map was not very accurate compared to the standards of Escher's world. The small representation of the observatory on its tor had been placed by someone who had only heard that there might be a building there. Escher had compensated as much as he could in locating the starting point of his line. Now he drew that line straight until it intersected the one he had previously marked. "The compass should be within a small radius of this point," he said, wondering if he should explain the uncertainties of measurement.

"That's assuming it wasn't moved between the two scryings."

Escher paused for a moment. "Yes, that's right. If we don't find the compass, we'll just take new measurements until we pin it down." She was even sharper than he had given her credit for.

"Thank you, I'll investigate immediately. If it doesn't turn up, I'll be in contact with you again to arrange a new scrying. Next time we can perform two scryings as close together as possible."

Escher had a strong premonition about this thing that Emeline desired. He wanted a chance to see it up close. "Might I suggest that I accompany you? This is more interesting than the usual recovery of a lost ring or a misplaced will that I'm typically called upon to find."

Emeline crossed her arms and looked away. "It's a family matter. I've already involved outsiders more than I would have preferred."

"I can assure you that I treat my clients with the utmost confidentiality and discretion. I have an inkling from the images that we saw that the compass may have been acquired by a collector or broker. I was an art dealer before coming here. I might be able to assist in negotiations."

Emeline had a skeptical eye. "What sort of art did you deal in, M. Resche?"

"Whatever my clients wanted."

She looked at Trefoil. "You trust him, do you?"

Trefoil tilted his head to consider this. "He's very dependable."

"I suppose that will do. Cats can sense who to trust. I'll take a cat's advice over a dog's any day, and over most people most days." Trefoil ran a paw over his whiskers a few times. Escher thought it was a little overdone.

Emeline turned to the door and called out, "Joseph!"

A man with shoulders nearly as broad as the door leaned in. He had only a fringe of hair, which accented the canted nose in the middle of the round face. His appearance and rude attire made Escher assume that she had summoned the foreman of the print shop, but she said, "Would you please finish editing the piece on Dr. Wolfe's expedition, then put together the gossip column from the notes I left? I'm going out for several hours."

"Certainly, Emeline. Do you need a bodyguard? Or a chaperone?" His tone said that both were unlikely.

"Bodyguard? Hmm, no. I haven't insulted anyone lately, at least not in print. I seem to have a chaperone already." She reached up to scratch Trefoil's ear.

"The paper will be on time, no worries. Don't do anything I wouldn't do."

"Why, Joseph, I don't think that rules out much besides the use of semicolons."

Joseph gave her a lopsided grin, gave a wave to Escher, and ducked out.

"Joseph is my assistant editor, and was too kind to say in front of strangers that the paper is more likely to be on time when I'm not here."

As they headed for the door, Escher ventured, "If you don't mind me asking, it seems unusual to allow employees to call you by your first name. Being a woman running a business in this town is tough enough; I would think that you wouldn't want your employees becoming overly familiar with you."

"But that's just it. If I insist on being Mademoiselle Cigne, I am advertising both my marital status, or lack thereof, and my family name, and anything I accomplish can be said to be because of that leverage. I'll run the business on a name that is solely mine. Real respect comes from more than a name and an honorific."

"I sympathize entirely."

They had reached the outer door and both reached for the knob. Escher almost stepped on her, then she tripped on his foot and he had to catch her. Embarrassed silence followed them down the street after they untangled themselves. Emeline attempted to break the ice again. "You said that you moved to town a year ago, M. Resche?"

Escher acknowledged that it was so.

"Where did you live before here? You said you were an art dealer?"

"I lived in a city called Geneva, by a lake surrounded by tall mountains. I was a thief."

Emeline missed a step in surprise. Escher continued, though he wasn't quite sure why. "Mostly, I stole things back for people who had been defrauded, cheated, or robbed themselves. It didn't make it any more legal, but I have a compulsion to steal things, and that made it more ethically acceptable, at least to me."

"Where is this Geneva?"

"It doesn't exist in this world. I walked into a fog one evening and came out the other side here in Plurs."

"So there *are* other worlds. Uncle Piers told me of a theory that such might exist, and hoped that he might find a crossing between them on his journeys. And you find one right here in the center of Plurs." Escher wondered why she believed him so readily.

"Unfortunately, it has proven to be a one-way crossing. I have been trying to find my way back ever since."

"If you're a thief … were you trying to steal something from Lady Moonbird while she is away?"

"No! I really am taking care of her place for her."

"Where has she gone, really?"

"She's buried under the rosebushes in the garden."

They both stopped in shock. Something was very wrong. Escher patted his jacket frantically, then plunged his hand into a pocket where a warm lump intruded that had not been there before. He pulled out a gold ring with a serpent engraved on the band that wove an intricate pattern three times around, ending with its tail in its mouth. It was hot to the touch. This time it wasn't something he had purloined; this had been planted.

"This is a Knot of Truth!"

"You killed Lady Moonbird," said Emeline in horror. She didn't shrink away from that horror, though. She squared her shoulders and faced him directly.

Think, don't react. Keep emotions in check. Turn a reversal to an advantage. He had schooled himself to those lessons, but it was so hard not to clench his fists and … no. He let the fury touch his eyes, just enough. Emeline took a step back and said, "This may not have been the best idea I ever had …"

Escher held up the ring. He had it; he could use it in his favor. "By this ring, I did not. It was another who did so because she gave me some information. I am going to bring that person down if I can." He placed the ring in her hand, closed her fingers over it, and held her fist closed with his own. It was now as hot to the touch as if it had been sitting in the afternoon sun for hours. "Now tell me, what's your game? Are you a Player?"

"I … I'm not sure what you mean by 'player.' I thought it was strange that you had taken Lady Moonbird's place, so I wanted to investigate. I was expecting to hear about a robbery or something, not … what you said."

"Is the compass real, or is it an entrapment?"

"No, it's real. I've been unable to find it through conventional means, so I made appointments with you and with Lady Moonbird. While I thought there was a slim chance that either of you would locate it for me, I thought at least I could do a story on how unscrupulous charlatans make their money by offering hope to those who have exhausted their own. I was surprised that you got such a definite location on it. The final test, of course, is if it's really where you say it is." Emeline's face twisted in discomfort. "Can you let go now? This ring is going to burn me if I hold it much longer."

Escher held her hand for another beat as he looked into her eyes. They were steady and direct. She was either telling the truth or was a superb liar. Her eyes were brown. If they had been green, he might have broken her hand. History.

He decided to take her explanation at face value. He released her hand and held the ring up to examine it; he almost dropped it. "Ah! You weren't kidding. Normally the Knots that I use vaporize after one use. The gold of the ring must be conducting the heat from the Knot, but there's a limit." He was deliberately sublimating his anger in his analysis of the ring, though the ring was a fascinating artifact in its own right. "Where did you get this?"

"From a jeweler named Metrophanes on the east side of town."

"Good to know. I'll be going now. Good luck with your compass."

"No, wait." Emeline chewed her lip. "I owe you an apology. I jumped to a conclusion without any evidence. Putting a Ring of Truth in your pocket was an underhanded move, and I'm sorry for that. You said you didn't kill her, but you know who did and that you want to see justice done. I'll help you with that. I want to find my compass before it is moved and we have to start the scryings all over again. You want to help with that. Would you agree to a provisional partnership?"

"Provisional," Escher agreed. "I've been betrayed by a partner in the past, and I would react badly if it were to happen again."

"I understand."

They resumed their course and soon arrived at the Square of the Booksellers. There were booksellers on the square, of course, but also stationers and apothecaries, as well as a quaint store selling brass reading lamps, named The Lampworks. But Escher suddenly felt quite confident that they would need to check only one store. Facing them was a small clockmaker's shop, with the brief legend in the window: M. Fourquereau, Prop.

Clock Shop

The Plurs Chasm

January 17, 1921 (from the archives)

An heiress is accused of concealing the will left by her late husband. Readers of this paper will remember that three years ago, it was reported that upon the death of Beaufort Warburton, his widow, Cecilia Warburton (née Singerly), produced a will that gave her sole control of the extensive Warburton estates. Shortly afterwards, a gentleman named Jules Charton took up residence in her household, among rumors that they had been romantically entangled for some years. M. Charton had a reputation as a mystic, and soon rumors swirled about unworldly rites that were performed in their mansion, and Mme Warburton began referring to herself as the "Lady of the West." Recently, a new will has come to light that would have transferred the bulk of the estate to Warburton's nephew, providing only a modest townhouse for the widow's usage until her death. A cover letter gave the reasons for these changes as Warburton's awareness of his wife's infidelity. The new will is contested by the widow as a forgery, throwing the entire matter into the Magistrate's court.

The man called Escher and the woman called Emeline Cigne pushed open the door to the clockmaker's shop. To say that a bell rang as the door opened was like saying that only one bird sang at sunrise. There was a tintinnabulation that would have made an Edgar Allen of this world scribble furiously with his quill in search of adjectives sufficiently recondite to capture the din. It was, Escher thought, quite overdone.

Fourquereau sat on a tall stool behind a counter. With his round face and drooping white mustaches, he looked like a clock himself, showing a time of forty minutes past four. There were clocks everywhere, on the walls, on shelves, on the counter, in display cases, and a half dozen great grandfather clocks standing on the floor. The room was filled with ticking as weights descended and clock springs unwound. Pendulums swung and governors spun and several anniversary clocks twirled under their glass domes. All the clocks agreed on the correct time — down to the second.

"M. Resche," acknowledged the clockmaker. "And, I believe, Mlle Cigne, though I've never had the pleasure. I recognize you from your picture in the newspaper."

"M. Fourquereau," said Escher, inclining his head.

"Indeed I am, M. Fourquereau," said Emeline. "How good of you to follow my paper. I believe we may have met briefly, in fact. I was visiting my Uncle Piers when you stopped by, some time ago. I was just a girl at the time."

"Ah, Piers Cigne. I had not made the connection. He would occasionally bring me exotic pieces from his travels." Escher felt sure that Fourquereau was less than truthful about several points in this statement.

Emeline took the cue smoothly. "I am seeking just such a small thing, a navigator's compass that my uncle left with his estate. He gave me to understand that he would leave it to me, but it seems to have been sold with his estate. With your interest in mechanisms, perhaps you would encounter such a thing?"

While Emeline was speaking, Escher's eye fell upon a clock behind Fourquereau that jarred him. It was an ordinary clock, weight-driven, with an unremarkable face. What disturbed Escher was that the clock was five minutes slow. He looked away to watch the clockmaker's expression.

Fourquereau put on the air of a man trying to recall a small detail. Escher sensed that he was deciding whether to tell the truth, a falsehood, or a misdirection. Escher closed his hand around a Knot in his pocket.

"I might have seen such a thing. Can you describe it to me?"

Emeline described it, as she had to Escher. "It is likely of no value, but it is of sentimental value to me. I would very much like to recover it."

"I might have seen such an item, though I mostly deal in clocks. Yes, a compass such as that was in a lot that I acquired at auction not long ago, though long enough that it slipped my mind."

The clock behind Fourquereau was disturbing Escher's concentration. His eye kept returning to its stubborn refusal to conform to the correct time.

"I would like to recover it. I'll pay you whatever you paid for it since it never should have been in the auction lot."

Fourquereau turned his hands out in a gesture of helplessness. "Alas, dear lady, it is promised to one of my clients. A promise made is a promise honored. I could not sell it back to you now." The Knot in Escher's pocket pulsed.

"Surely, you could obtain another navigator's compass for your client?"

"Unfortunately, Mademoiselle, your uncle had a reputation in certain circles. I do not know this for a fact, but now that you tell me the origin of the piece, I think that provenance is what my client valued. I could not substitute another."

Escher yanked his eyes away from the errant clock one more time. His Knot remained quiet.

"Could you tell me the name of your client? Perhaps I can appeal to him or her to relinquish any claim promised, or perhaps I can bid a higher price for its return."

"Regrettably, my client's name must remain confidential. I'm sure you understand. You would not reveal your client's names to me." Escher's Knot pulsed ambiguously and began to crumble in his hand. It was nearly used up.

"Then, if nothing else, please convey my interest to your client. Please appeal to sentiment, or fairness, or if nothing else, pecuniary interest to return this trinket to Piers' nearest living relative."

"That, at least, I can promise you. It makes me happy that you found a small way that I can render assistance."

"Very well, then, Monsieur. We shall be going. Everyone knows where to find me — at the newspaper office."

"A moment," interrupted Escher. "I wonder if you can tell me why that one clock, out of all of the clocks in this room, is not telling the correct time?"

Fourquereau smiled. "And how do you know that's not the correct time and all the other clocks are fast? Must the majority always be right and the outlier wrong? Or perhaps the clock is telling the right time and is simply in the wrong place? It might be the correct time of another place than this."

Escher looked hard at him. "Sometimes, a slow clock is simply a slow clock, not a puzzle."

Fourquereau beamed like a mustached buddha receiving a koan from a student. "Sometimes, it is."

Escher and Emeline let themselves out to another tumult of bells. He took her arm in a cordial way and guided her to a nearby open-air cafe. He asked her recommendation for tea, ordered for both of them, and scandalized the waiter and

Emeline by requesting cream. They said little until they had been served and the waiter withdrew.

"I hadn't realized until just now," said Emeline, "that we hadn't discussed terms or payments for your services."

Escher set the cream in front of a third chair at their table. "You'll have to take that up with my business manager." A silver-grey cloud drifted in from the potted plants that defined the cafe's boundaries on the square. Trefoil materialized in the empty chair and sampled the cream appreciatively.

"Ah, I see. Well, M. Chat? What price would you put on your companion's services?"

Trefoil looked speculatively at her. "I believe that he might consider himself well compensated by a dinner at a quiet place with dim lighting and a good bottle of wine."

"Trefoil!"

Emeline looked amused. "That might be arranged."

"And also, you could send around some whitefish to our place …"

"Hmm. Do you like mackerel?"

"Rawr!"

"Well, then. Done." She turned to Escher. "What did you think of the clockmaker's story?"

Escher was trying not to show his discomfort. He had tossed out the quip about Trefoil acting as his business manager, and Trefoil had turned the tables on him. The cat had a smug set to his whiskers as he lapped up his cream. Escher swallowed as he collected his thoughts to reply.

"It was interesting. I had a Knot of Veracity in my pocket. It's a bit different from a Knot of Truth, which compels the holder to tell the truth. This Knot tells the holder if another is telling a falsehood or a truth. He was truthful that he had seen it, and that it has value, and that he won't return it to you. He didn't tell any lies. However, when he said that he had promised it to a client, the Knot was silent. Somehow that statement was ambiguous. But the upshot remains, he's unwilling to give you or sell you your compass."

"Hmm. Interesting."

"Trefoil, what did you see?"

"Wait, where was he?" asked Emeline. "I didn't see him."

"You wouldn't," said Trefoil complacently. "The compass is in his back room, in a locked display case along with several other instruments. I'm fairly certain there are some topomantic wards around the case and perhaps some traps as well. These are objects that he values and protects well."

"Interesting."

Emeline inquired, "What was that banter about the one slow clock?"

"Probably nothing. I can't bear things that are out of place, or that violate the pattern that they're in. I usually make that obsession work for me in, uh, my line of work. Sometimes it's just a distraction. If Fourquereau knew about my quirk, he might have been exploiting it to distract me from what he was saying. I don't think he knows that about me, though. It probably was, as he said, just a slow clock." Escher told himself that he was still talking too much.

Emeline finished her tea thoughtfully and put the cup down. "M. Resche — Maurits — would you do something for me?"

Escher found his heart suddenly beating hard.

"What do you have in mind?"

"Would you steal the compass for me?"

Escher kept his face impassive as he frantically calculated the possible responses to this question. He was becoming convinced that this compass was one of the artifacts used in the Game and, as such, one that could channel or direct geomantic energy. It could be crucial for returning him home. He could decline and attempt to steal it anyway. He could agree but tell her that he failed in the attempt. He could do the deed and try to find out how the device worked. He could tell her his plan and hope she helped him. Which would benefit him the most?

He rejected the option of failing, or appearing to. Pride forbade it. If he declined and she went back to Fourquereau and found it stolen, she would suspect him immediately. If he agreed, he could decide later about doing private experimentation or enlisting her help. That option would give him the most flexibility, he decided. It wasn't because the prospect of continuing to work with Emeline appealed to him. He didn't make decisions that way.

She was watching him from across the cafe table. He wondered if she regretted the impulse that had made her ask that. Perhaps there was a way to feel out her willingness to help him.

"I'll do it. Maybe there is some research you can help me with in turn."

Her eyes showed a hint of wariness. "What would that be?"

"Would you care to accompany me to the symphony tomorrow evening?"

The silence while she digested this stretched painfully. Escher wondered why he cared. He could go alone.

Emeline said quietly, "I'm not sure what sort of research you are pursuing, but I'd enjoy going to the symphony with you."

He managed a smile, though inwardly he was telling himself that this was a bad idea after all. "I'm glad. It should be a good program." He had no clue what the program was, but the local symphony did have a good reputation.

"Since your manager has negotiated compensation for your services, let me take you to dinner before the concert. Shall we say Robillard's at 6? That's close to the *Salle*; we'll have ample time to have a leisurely meal."

"Let's meet at the restaurant at six, then." Emeline stood to leave. After an instant, Escher stood as well. It was how things were done here.

As he watched Emeline walk down the street in the direction of the newspaper office, he muttered to himself, "Actually, that sounds terrifying."

Trefoil twitched his tail. "I arranged it so you can go through all the complicated rituals that you humans go through. Cats have it much easier. We just find an alley or a rooftop and fornicate."

"That's not what I had in mind!"

"Of course it is, you just don't know it yet."

Symphony

The Plurs Chasm

May 19, 2008

Captain Reilly, of the police station on the Street of the Pawnbrokers, is looking for policeman Dennis O'Connell. The man was paid at the station house yesterday afternoon. Later in the day, his keys and shield were found near the Square of the Publicans. This has led to the belief that O'Connell has gone off on a drunk. His fellow officers are inclined to believe that the young officer's violent temper drove him to drink. Disinterested people who have noticed his conduct of late are not so charitable. Unless he shows up in two days, he will probably be dismissed from the force.

The man who had given the name M. Resche to the maître d' hotel sat at the table by the garden window at Robillard's, nervously glancing at the clock on the wall. He had arrived ten minutes early to be sure of a good table where he could see the room, have his back to the wall, and keep his eye on the clock. Like the waiters, the clock was elegant and patient and made sure that you knew that it was there. Its steady ticking had gravitas, as if assuring you that the wines in the cellar were growing steadily older and better and more expensive.

Now the hands of the clock had only the last interval to cross before the hour. Escher counted the tables in the room once more — seventeen — and the chairs — forty-eight — and found three ways in which the tables could be arranged more efficiently, two of which would allow an eighteenth table, and four ways in which the arrangement would have a more pleasing symmetry. He was just beginning to enumerate the wine bottles in their bins when the tall form of Emeline appeared in the doorway. The maître d' greeted her by name and conducted her at once to Escher's table. She was dressed in a blue gown that was elegant of cut and snug of fit, off one shoulder to display the side of her long neck and her graceful collarbones. Escher barely remembered to stand as the maître d' held the chair for Emeline.

"You look lovely tonight," he said as they sat. Somehow he felt that wasn't adequate, but Emeline dimpled with a smile. He wished he had more confidence, the way he had briefly felt when he had constructed the persona to deal with Hesperia. Immediately, he regretted thinking of that incident. He didn't want to be that way with anyone (with the possible exception of evil witches in demon-infested castles), and most especially with Emeline, whose respect he was inexplicably interested in retaining. He would just have to be himself this evening, which was to say, awkward.

"You're very dashing, yourself," she replied. Escher was wearing a maroon coat, a cream vest, and a cravat of crimson. It was the only formal evening wear in his size at the men's store that afternoon, and at that, there were a couple of pins to get it to fit to the satisfaction of the tailor. (One in the side seam jabbed him at inopportune moments.) The proprietor had almost not let him out of the store without proper alterations, but Escher had promised to bring it in for finishing after it had served its purpose this evening.

"I met Trefoil outside. A shame he couldn't come in with us, but they're a little stuffy about such things here. I told him to go around back, and I asked the staff to leave some fish tails outside the door for him."

"That was very thoughtful of you."

A waiter brought two flutes of champagne on a silver tray, placing them before Emeline and Escher with a flourish. Escher raised an eyebrow.

"I asked Sébastien to follow his whim this evening," said Emeline, reaching for her glass. "I believe he does his own special variation of scrying to determine the dishes that will please each particular customer, and comes up with some exquisite combinations." She raised her glass. "To your health!"

Escher raised his. "And to yours!" He felt disquieted that he might be the subject of someone's scrying at a time like this, even for such a limited inquiry as divining his tastes in food. What other facts could those preferences leak about him?

"Is something concerning you?" Emeline had picked up his slight hesitation.

"No. Well, a bit. I haven't been on a date in years. And, as I told you, I'm not the most socially — what is the opposite of inept? Is ept a word? — of people."

Emeline smiled. "Would you rather do as your cat suggests and find a dark alley or a rooftop, and, as he so delicately puts it, f—"

"He said that to you? I'll wring his little neck."

"Don't be hard on him. I was amused. He's a cat; that's how he thinks. I'm a woman; I like our little social rituals, even if they *might* have the same goal in mind."

Escher was reassured for a brief second until the import of what Emeline had just said sank in. He was just starting to gape at her when the waiter swept up to their table. "For mademoiselle, a small salad of quail eggs nesting in cress with capers and a light raspberry drizzle, and a glass of Terres Blanches Robert. For monsieur, a small cup of savory soup with beans and crispy pork, and a glass of Domaine Bertrand vin rouge. Bon appétit."

Escher was forced to admit to himself that he had lost control of the evening. Also that, to his surprise, he was enjoying it.

At first, Emeline talked of the town's gossip, the small scandals and petty politics that any town kept hidden. These were not normally of interest to Escher, but Emeline told them in an engaging and entertaining way. During the interlude between courses, however, Emeline casually turned the conversation in an unexpected direction. "I've always loved tales of other lands. Uncle Piers crossed the chasms into faraway geogons. He told me of vast seas of ice, and steamy jungles, and deserts and mountains. But you came from a geogon that isn't even in this world. What's it like?"

Escher thought about how to answer this. He had told few of his origin, and none in any detail, so he didn't have a practiced story. "First of all, we don't call them geogons, because the earth's surface hasn't been jumbled like a puzzle. You have to cross half the world to get to those mountains that are to our west, not just cross a chasm. Everything was the same up until the early 1600s, but then the Geography Disaster occurred in this world. My world didn't have the wars and famines that followed the Disaster; we had a different set of wars. Science advanced more quickly there. We have cars — like carriages — that move without horses, and ships that fly through the sky." He talked much more than he thought he would. They were almost late in leaving for the symphony.

❖

It was a short stroll to *le Salle Communale*, where the orchestra would perform. The last few people were hurrying inside as they arrived, and Escher gave his name to the head usher. They were conducted up the grand stairs.

"That was a memorable dinner," said Escher. "Thank you for suggesting it." He was slightly unsteady on his feet due to the excellent wine that had accompanied each course, which was much more than the single sherry that he typically allowed himself in an evening. It gave Emeline an excuse to put her arm through his to steady him.

The usher opened a door for them. "Oh, Maurits, you got a private box! How extravagant!"

"Nearly as much as you just spent on that dinner," he affirmed. "I'm not sure that we can afford each other."

"We can eat soup and cold porridge for a week to make up for it," she said. "With our own box, we could have smuggled Trefoil in instead of leaving him out on the streets."

"He'll be happier outside. Music bores him, and he knows the backdoors of the best restaurants in the area. He'll be fine."

"Oh, they're starting. Shh."

The tuning-up sounds of the orchestra died away. Into the silence walked the conductor, Helka Aaltonen. She bowed once, turned to the orchestra, and raised her baton. She let the tension build for long seconds, then launched into Mozart's Flute and Harp Concerto. Escher considered himself very much ignorant of music; his gifts and obsessions focused on the visual and the topological. Whenever he found himself in a conversation in which music was discussed, he felt himself at sea on a torrent of unfamiliar terms and concepts, as if he had wandered into a foreign land. Now he closed his eyes and listened to the patterns that filled the air, the high, pure voices of the flute and harp dancing around each other, mirroring and echoing one another, filling the space of the *Salle* with beauty.

Too soon, it was over. Escher opened his eyes to join in the enthusiastic applause, to find Emeline watching him with a small smile of amusement.

"The music really took you away, didn't it?"

"Humph. How do you know I wasn't asleep"?"

"Your eyes were closed, but you had a look of intense concentration on your face. Also, your fingers were moving in time with the music. I could tell that you were listening. Why did you close your eyes? I like to watch the performers as I listen."

"I can't hear as well if I'm seeing, and I can't see as well if I'm listening. Or smelling or tasting. It's hard to describe. I'm driven to focus on what I'm doing."

Emeline smiled, "You're a remarkable person." She turned to add her hands to the sound of the applause that swelled like a summer downpour on the roof as the soloists took another bow.

There was no intermission, but the orchestra moved directly into the Mozart Clarinet Concerto in A Major. Again Escher was caught up in the patterns of the music. He likened it to an aural mandala, drawing the ear through carefully curling arcs and shadings to that quiet place of self-awareness. He knew that Mozart lived after the time of the Geography Disaster, though he was hazy about exactly when. He reflected on the coincidence that both time streams had produced this genius when they had diverged in so many other ways. He opened his eyes again to find Emeline watching him. He smiled — a little self-consciously — and she snuggled closer and turned her eyes to watch the performers. He found his hand clasped in hers, and that was fine.

❖

After the end of the program, the holders of box seats were invited to a reception with the conductor and soloists. That was, after all, the reason that Escher had purchased those seats. While the box holders and other patrons were an exclusive crowd, they still outnumbered the principal performers by a substantial margin. While Escher awaited a chance to speak to Aaltonen, they circulated among the other guests. Escher knew few of the other concertgoers and none really well enough to strike up a conversation with them. Emeline, on the other hand, knew many of them. And not, it seemed, in her capacity of newspaper publisher. Many asked after her parents, or this uncle or that aunt. She only replied in generalities, but Escher began to suspect that she might have more standing in the community than she had let him believe. A few had apparently been on the receiving end of her reporting and were frostily polite. Through her, Escher met and exchanged pleasantries with the Mayor, the Bishop, a rabbi, the Dean of the local university, several minor lords and ladies, and …

"Ah, Lord Molendinarii, allow me to introduce you to my good friend …"

"Escher," a voice hissed.

Escher turned and hastily put on his best poker face — the one he wore when he had only two pair and suspected he was facing a full house. "You must have mistaken me for someone else, sir. I do not believe I have yet had the pleasure of your acquaintance." Molendinarii scowled, an expression that Escher had seen before and which frequently haunted his dreams.

Emeline intervened, though not without a puzzled glance at Escher. "This is Monsieur Resche, my lord, a scryer whom I recently had occasion to consult. I then discovered we shared a number of interests, music among them."

"Indeed. I'm not surprised you" — a hint of a sneer here — "would have common interests with someone I last found in my vault with a surprising array of topomantic lock-picking tools, with one of my prized possessions in his hand. And *you* —" He looked at Emeline. "I thought journalist was *one* step above a thief, but I may be wrong. It's fortunate that your grandparents are no longer alive to watch you trash your family name."

Emeline rocked back at that as if she'd been slapped. She went on the attack. "If it comes to that, Lord Molendinarii, you wouldn't be the person that the Magistrate is looking for in connection with a recent murder, would you? I'm sure she would be interested in a lead provided by a journalist who had become known for sending three corrupt nobles to prison in the past year."

Molendinarii snarled, turned on his heel and strode from the room.

Reception

The Plurs Chasm

January 4, 1901 (from the archives)

Book Review: "The Secrete Log-Boke of Christopher Columbus," written by Himself.

This is one of the most clever and artistic conceits that has appeared in a long time. It is a facsimile of a logbook purporting to have found on the English coast a few months ago. The text is in old Gothic, the leaves in parchment, and the entries are decorated by illustrations such as a sailor might have made. The effect of reality is marred only by the text being in English …

"We'd better go as well, 'Escher,' " said Emeline tightly. "I wouldn't put it past him to arrange a surprise for us on the way home."

"We can't go yet, I want to talk to the Meisterin."

"Whatever for?"

"There's a certain musical instrument — a Pythagorean Harp — that I want to find out about."

"Was … that the entire point of the evening, then?"

"Yes … No. Yes, a box seat was a means to a ticket to the reception. No, it wasn't the entire point. I didn't want to go alone, but … I enjoyed both dinner and the concert more than I expected to."

"You didn't expect to enjoy my company?"

"No! This isn't coming out right." Escher took a deep breath. "I have this fear that if I let someone too close, they might find out I'm just an act papered over an awkward and obsessed person. That's a quote from a former therapist, by the way."

"I disagree with this 'therapist,' whatever that is. You have an interesting way of looking at things, if sometimes confusing. Putting that aside, though, I'm disturbed that you didn't tell me you had made an enemy of Molendinarii. You endangered both of us by walking around town openly. You're just lucky we encountered him where there are too many people for him to act. I would have taken more precautions had I known."

"It's me that he wants. You're not in any danger from him."

"Did that help Lady Moonbird? It *was* Molendinarii who killed her, wasn't it? The pieces are fitting together."

Escher was silent.

"I thought we had a partnership. That should include keeping each other safe and informed."

"Do you have the Ring of Truth? I want to be sure you believe me."

"I do, but I don't need it. The ring has limitations. It doesn't let you say something that you know is false, but you can remain silent unless asked directly. You can even reply with something true but misleading. Right now, I don't want truth, I want sincerity."

Escher took a deep breath. "Very well. You called yourself 'professionally nosy,' though I think it's more fair to say that you can't resist a mystery. I kept quiet about this at first because I didn't know you, and then because I didn't want to involve you in this mess. It didn't occur to me that I was endangering you just by proximity. I probably wasn't putting you at risk until this evening when we were seen in public at the restaurant and the symphony. But you're right, Molendinarii could try to get leverage over me by threatening you." Escher reached out and took her hand. "It would work, too."

She didn't appear entirely mollified by this. "Do what you came to do and let's get out of here."

She had no sooner said this when a small voice behind him said, "M. Chesrè?"

Escher tried to keep his face impassive but was unable to avoid a small tick of the eyes towards the speaker. Emeline sighed. Caught out, Escher turned and tried to make the best of it. The young harpist from the Daughters' refuge stood behind him, a shy smile on her face. What was her name? Mia, wasn't it? "I saw you here and I wanted to thank you again. I have been taken on to study with the Meisterin. If I study hard, I have a chance at a place in the orchestra. I wanted to tell you that you do so much in helping the Daughters of the Road. You must be a very good person."

"All I do is give people a chance. What they do with it is up to them. I'm glad you are making the most of your opportunity."

"I'm happy you have helped give me that opportunity. Good night." She melted away in the crowd.

"Well, that was … interesting," said Emeline. "Don't think that it has escaped me that all of your names are anagrams. Are any of them real?"

"What's in a name? A rose …"

"Remember how the deception in that play ended? Ask yourself if you want to complete that quotation."

Escher chose silence while they waited.

The crowd had thinned by then, and it wasn't much longer before Aaltonen was free for a moment.

"Good evening, Meisterin. We enjoyed the performance tonight," said Emeline as they approached. Aaltonen was exceedingly tall, had a pale complexion, and light, flaxen hair that she wore trimmed short. A warm smile offset the otherwise ice queen aspect her color lent her.

"Thank you, Mlle Cigne. It's good to see you again. Was your usual music columnist not available this evening?"

"As it happens, I'm not here in a professional capacity. I'm on a date." Emeline said this with a smile that belied her current annoyance with Escher. "This is M. Resche, a local scryer of impressive skill."

Escher bowed. "Pleased to make your acquaintance, Meisterin. That harp and flute were magnificent. I could just see the notes dancing in the air, like a battalion of fireflies soaring over a rushing stream in the moonlight. They repeated and interlocked and mirrored each other like a great tessellation of sound. Tell me what magic you use to induce such visions."

Aaltonen looked pleased but bemused. "No magic, other than the notes themselves, and Mozart's genius in arranging them in beautiful ways. I think if they gave rise to visions, that tells us more about your own mind than about the music."

"I suppose I am quite visual. It is a necessary qualification in my field of endeavor. Is there no musical equivalent to topomancy, then?" This was, he hoped, a leading question. It had an even quicker payoff than he could have wished for.

"There is a field of harmonurgy, but it's difficult to use in performance, not to mention wildly unethical. Our modern scales are not well suited to it. It's best performed with older instruments such as the Pythagorean Harp."

"I've never heard of such a thing."

"I have several in my collection of harps at my home. They are not true harps in the style that you saw tonight, and are played quite differently. They are tuned with moveable bridges on a scale that derives each note mathematically from the previous. However, this doesn't quite complete an octave, so there is a gap, termed a 'comma,' before the next octave. The result is a very pleasing scale, but not one that is suited to symphonic pieces."

"How does that lend itself to harmonurgy?" asked Escher.

"Pythagoras believed that an instrument tuned to this scale would allow the player to perceive the structure of reality. He called it the principle of Divine Harmony, and he felt so strongly about it that he wrote that music should never be used for mere entertainment because it was too powerful to use frivolously."

"Is there anything to that?" asked Emeline.

"There are some local mystics who dabble in it. Perhaps you could ask them if you are looking for a story. Lady Moonbird is the one who has usually borrowed it, though this time it was M. Tanylive, the Apothecary."

"Oh, they're meeting soon?"

"I believe so. He arranged to pick it up four days from today."

"Thank you for the lead. That might make for a very colorful story."

They took their leave, collected their cloaks at the exit, and went out into the streets.

"Was that easy?" asked Emeline after a while.

"Not really. I hate receptions."

"I mean telling a lie. Saying that you had never heard of a Pythagorean Harp when that's exactly what you were looking for."

"Oh. I ... Well, I couldn't just walk up to her and say that, could I?"

"I think you could have if you tried. But you did what came naturally to you."

"It didn't harm anyone ..." His protest was cut short.

"Hiss! I heard something up ahead." Trefoil had appeared in the shadows.

"That was fast. Could Molendinarii have put someone on us that quickly?"

"I suggest we not wait to find out."

They cut left on a side street to reach a wider avenue, but it was still deserted, with all the shops closed for the night. They started walking but froze when a clatter came from a dark alley.

"Do you have any weapons?" asked Emeline. There might have been some fear in her eyes, but she didn't let it show in her voice, which was as calm as before.

"I have a Knot of Confusion, and a mandala that would probably give someone a dreadful headache — or possibly cure one they already had. After that, I'm out. How about you?"

"I have a Press card and a Ring of Truth. Not much help, I'm afraid."

"Personally, I find both of those pretty scary. We'd better keep walking."

For the next ten streets or so, they walked briskly, peering into darkened doorways and jumping at small noises. At many points, Escher was convinced that someone was lurking in the shadows, but if there was, the unknown person confined his activity to lurking. Any competent stalker would have been quieter, leading him to think the point might just be to instill fear in them. Or — just possibly — it was the normal noises of rats and drunks shuffling out of sight, and their imaginations were supplying the sinister intentions. When the neighborhood transitioned from commercial to residential, the threatening shadows seemed to lift.

They came soon to Emeline's modest townhouse. A few lights shown in the neighbor's windows. It had a safe feeling after the fright they had given themselves in the darker parts of town. By now, they were convinced that it was just a case of nerves and were joking about how frightened they had been.

They faced each other before the door. "Well, goodnight," said Escher awkwardly.

"Goodnight. I enjoyed the evening. I would invite you in, but … I need to think about what I've learned tonight." She gave him a quick peck on the cheek and vanished within while he was still too floored to respond.

After a long moment, Escher turned to make his way back to the observatory. A grey shadow joined him. "So, how was the evening?" asked Trefoil.

Escher shook his head. "I am still trying to figure that out."

Jeweler

𝔈𝔥𝔢 ℜ𝔩𝔲𝔯𝔰 ℭ𝔥𝔞𝔰𝔪

May 19, 1999 (from the archives)

The intrepid explorer Piers Cigne has again re-turned home from a new land that has been lost for so many centuries that it is widely regarded as a legend. The land of America was still a dark and largely unexplored continent at the time of the Geography Disaster. A few years before the disaster, reports had come back of a titanic waterfall, far beyond anything familiar to our readers, that emptied an entire lake over its brink each and every day. This magnificent waterfall has never been found again after the disaster, but now M. Cigne has once more found the way. To reach that land, he entered a valley that until recently had been covered edge to edge with a glacier, and upon traversing it to the end, beheld a sight thought lost forever. This was news to the people who he found living there, of course, who were only too glad to resupply the travelers with the bounty that grew near the waters …

Metrophanes the jeweler had a shop, not in the avenue of jewelers as might be expected, but on the street of the pawn-brokers. Yet, as Escher and Trefoil watched surreptitiously over several hours, a surprisingly well-dressed clientele for this part of town passed through his door with great regularity. A distinctly different class of person entered the pawnbroker's next door. The two sets of patrons studiously ignored each other.

At last, there appeared to be no customers in the jeweler's shop. Escher entered, leaving Trefoil to conduct surveillance. He was greeted by an altogether more eclectic inventory than he would have expected. Jewelry in a wide variety of styles fought for shelf space with elbows and insults. Quality varied as much as style: understated pearl chokers tried to ignore gaudy bracelets that wanted to put your eyes out. There was a curtained door to a back room that billowed suddenly just as Escher heard the door to the pawnshop close through the thin wall. Suddenly he understood.

Metrophanes emerged from an office cubby at one side. He was small of stature and wide of shoulder. His head and jaw were shaven, and golden hoops hung from his generous earlobes. Escher would have identified him as Mediterranean in his own world, but geography was a more complex subject here. "I am Metrophanes, the proprietor. May I help you?" he asked, in a tone Escher knew well. It meant that more could be offered to one who knew how to phrase the request.

"I am M. Resche, a scryer. I'm, ah, looking for a small piece for a friend. Nothing ostentatious. Perhaps a pendant."

"A close friend?"

"More of a business associate."

"And what would you like to say to this associate?"

"I would like to persuade her to … contribute to a venture."

"I will assemble a selection that might suit your purpose. Take a look around while I do that and let me know if you find anything else that catches your eye. Most of my pieces are consignments from other artists, but these two cases have my own creations."

Escher took a cursory look at the other shelves but quickly gravitated towards the works of Metrophanes. There were works in gold and in silver, and also in more exotic metals. There were crystals, pieces of amber, and a carving that might have been bone. Many of them were similar in style to Emeline's Ring. Very similar. In fact, among them, was another Ring of Truth, twin to the one he had already seen.

Metrophanes returned with five pendants, all of which were tasteful and would serve the stated purpose. He held them up one at a time for Escher's appreciation. One appeared to be Metrophanes' own work, which gave Escher an idea.

"This one is very nice, and my associate has a ring in a similar style," he said, placing his finger on a ring in the case — not the one containing the Knot of Truth, but another of similar style. "It might please her to have a matching set."

"It might at that," said Metrophanes. "All of these rings have twists of platinum filament hidden inside them during casting. The one you've indicated has a Knot that enhances the wearer's attractiveness. This pendant conveys a barely perceptible glow or aura about a person that has a similar effect. The two should reinforce each other." The jeweler smiled. "Perhaps you should not add this to her arsenal unless you have a suitable countermeasure?"

"You have such a thing?"

"Oh, yes. This ring next to it heightens your ability to see things as they truly are."

"Hmm. So all of your creations have topomantic enhancements to them?"

"Most do. It is what I am known for. This one increases your resistance to disease. This one increases your capacity for drink, or perhaps I should say it decreases the effect of that drink on your mental state. The hangovers are still your responsibility. The next one increases vigor and libido, and that one maintains a youthful appearance as you age. These last two are the most potent: the first will make those you deal with more likely to trust you, and the second compels the bearer to tell the truth."

Escher affected surprise. "Where is the advantage to that? Who would go around all day blurting out their secrets?"

"Its primary use is in consummating deals. Each party dons the ring in turn and recites his responsibilities and intentions. It's the one artifact in which you can see the Knot on the surface of the ring; this is to help guard against it being abused by the unscrupulous."

"Fascinating. I think that pendant is just what I'm looking for. How much is it?"

Metrophanes wrote some numbers on a slip of paper and proffered it to Escher.

"I see. Well, it seems worth the outlay. May I also inquire about the price of the 'countermeasure' ring?"

Metrophanes added another figure to the slip of paper. This one had more digits than the previous one.

"Ah. Any discount for a package deal?"

"I'm afraid not."

"Then, not today for the ring, I regret to say.'

Escher placed several hefty coins on the velvet pad on the counter. "While you get change, may I inspect the ring with the Knot of Perception?" Metrophanes opened the case and placed the ring on the velvet with such an assured demeanor that Escher knew that there were protections against any sleight of hand with which he might have tried to acquire the ring for himself. As the jeweler went to the back room to get change and to select a box for the pendant, Escher looked around the shop while ostensibly inspecting the ring. Most of the shop appeared unchanged with the ring in hand, as did the shopkeeper. Several of the display pieces that were allegedly consignments could be seen to be less — and in one case, more — than they appeared to be. Satisfied that the ring worked and wishing that he could acquire it, he placed the ring back on the counter as Metrophanes returned.

"Here you go, Monsieur." The jeweler displayed the contents of the box, so Escher could verify there had been no substitution. He then fixed Escher with a searching gaze. "You know your Knots, I see."

Escher hastily rewound the last few minutes and realized he had called the Knot of Perception by its true name. He shrugged, still holding the ring. "Several types of Knots are tools of my trade. I've made it my business to learn about a number of others to some degree. By the way, if you're interested in old artifacts, I've just heard that Fourquereau the clockmaker has acquired a compass formerly owned by Piers Cigne, the explorer."

"What of it? It is something more suited to a tinkerer like that old fool than an artisan such as myself."

Escher had put down the Ring of Perception, but still he knew that Metrophanes was much more interested than his words indicated. Tucking his purchase into a pocket in his cloak, he exited, meeting up with Trefoil outside. "So what's your next step?" asked Trefoil after Escher filled him in. "Wait for Metrophanes to steal the compass so you can buy or steal it from him?"

"He's probably not a thief himself. If he wants it badly enough, he'll commission one of his 'suppliers' to procure it for him. It's still early; I think I'll spend some time muddying the waters."

Two streets away, still in the district of pawnbrokers and smoke shops, Escher turned into another storefront. The proprietor was a slightly plump man with an oval face, a five o'clock shadow before noon, and a hairline that was not so much receding as it was in full and craven retreat. He was the sort of person who would sweat in an ice storm, so he continually mopped his neck with a handkerchief. His name was Edwards and he came from an English-speaking island to the west. He broke into a smile when he saw his customer enter. "M. Garnier! How nice to see you again. Has your aunt left you another set of jewelry that you would prefer in a lighter and quieter form?"

Escher had thought of pawning the pendant that he had just purchased to cover his visit to the jeweler, but on impulse decided now to hang on to it. Perhaps it *would* make a nice gift for Emeline. Instead, he said, "Actually, today I am looking for a timepiece. I lost my previous one and have been missing it. I thought I would start looking for a replacement."

"I don't have much selection, but there are one or two nice pieces." Edwards pulled out a tray from under his counter and extracted a pocket watch, which he placed on a pad of worn green velvet. Escher picked it up to examine it. The watch had an ornate silver case, with a lid that sprung open when a tab was pressed. Within, it had dials for the hour and minute and second, as well the day of the week and month. The markings were in ornate Roman numerals that were difficult to read. Beyond being the sort of watch that he would not only never carry but would try to lose at the first opportunity, there was a faint Finder spell engraved in the case. It was probably too weak to worry Edwards, but Escher wanted to carry nothing of the sort.

"Not quite what I'm looking for," he said, quickly ridding himself of the timepiece. "I'm a simpler sort of person."

"Sure you are, Monsieur." Edwards winked at him. "How about this one, then?"

This was a larger watch, without a hinged cover, in simple gold. He wound the stem at the top and watched the hands begin their stately measurement. The numerals on the face were large and easy-to-read, the hands were unostentatious. He unscrewed the glass cover to find the small lever that allowed him to set the time, then replaced the cover. Turning it over, he unscrewed the back, to find a second dust cover underneath. Within that cover he found a glistening mechanism, running smoothly on twenty-seven jeweled bearings, each gear turning at its assigned pace.

"It is a railroad watch, Monsieur. Perhaps a little too workman-like for a person such as yourself."

"And yet there is an attractive simplicity to it. It's not what I'm looking for, not at all like the one I lost, but I … I would give you two crowns for it."

"Two! Surely it is worth at least ten! Look at the gold in the casing."

Escher knew that Edwards would have asked more than twenty if he had been allowed to name the first price. They haggled for a while, then settled on five crowns just before Escher was ready to walk with an offer of seven on the table that Edwards said that he couldn't possibly better. "Oh, you're a thief, you are," said Edwards, earning him a sharp look from Escher. Edwards held up his hands. "Not in the literal sense, I am sure! But you drive a hard bargain. I'll be eating bread crusts for a week because of this deal. But you've brought me some nice pieces in the past that have made me a tidy profit, so I'll forgo my usual margin on this one. But if you come into any more inheritances, you bring them here first. Deal?"

Escher agreed and paid for his purchase. He declined any box for the watch, pocketing it instead. He wasn't sure yet why he had acquired it, other than admiration for the workmanship. As he was leaving, he said, apparently as an afterthought. "Timepieces. That reminds me. When I visited the clockmaker yesterday, he didn't have any watches that I wanted, but he did have a compass that he was doting over. He said that it had belonged to the adventurer Piers Cigne as if it would mean something to me. Does that ring any bells for you?"

Edwards said that it did not, but Escher saw his eye twitch as he spoke.

In the next few hours, he visited shops where he was known as Moulder, Harper, and Lesueur. He didn't buy anything at these places, though he used similar diversions to mention the compass in passing.

"How do you keep all those names straight?" asked Trefoil. "And what if one of them sees you about town or comes to consult you?"

"For the first, I have a good memory. For the second, it's useful to have an unremarkable appearance. People often forget what I look like, and I enhance that tendency by carrying a Knot of Seeming. It makes me resemble someone else whom they trust, so each of them would give you a different description."

"You always look the same to me."

"I suppose that means that you trust me. Seriously, though, I only activate it when I need it. In everyday life, it could lead to awkward situations."

"It might have been safer if you had used it with Lord Molendinarii."

"An adept of his level would have seen right through it, and even tipped him off that I was hiding something."

"So now what? Half the town is going to try to break into Fourquereau's shop?"

"Maybe not, but word will get around, and there will be too many suspects. Let's go back to the Observatory now and wait for night to fall."

Theft

The Plurs Chasm

June 1, 2014

The Editorial Board of the Plurs Chasm is pleased to report that the newspaper has been acquired by Mlle Emeline Cigne. Mlle Cigne is assuming the post of managing editor, effective with this edition, promising a new era of professional and investigative journalism. We wish to emphasize that this is a private venture for our new editor, and is in no way backed by or beholden to the interests of the Cigne family or estates.

The man who called himself Escher stood in the shadows near the shop of the clockmaker. He held the Knot that made him uninteresting, so attempts to lurk, skulk, slink, or prowl were unnecessary, and would in fact call attention to himself, negating the effects of the Knot. The cat who called himself something unpronounceable did some lurking, but since this is normal for cats, it was also uninteresting.

The Square of the Booksellers had more people about in the early evening than many parts of town. The cafes attracted people bound to or from nearby Playwright Road, where the theaters were located. However, passersby took no more notice of Escher than they did of a nearby trash bin. Later in the evening, an individual dressed in worn and probably second-hand clothing came by and tried the door on Fourquereau's shop. She dropped the handle hastily after the briefest touch and backed away with terror on her face. She bolted in the direction of lower town and didn't return.

As night deepened and the cafes closed, Escher departed his shadow. He passed near the shop's front door, holding his hand near the door handle. He could feel the prickles of a protection that had been laid on the lock, which would make anyone touching it see what they most feared. Escher knew his fear and had no desire to see that particular face again, so he kept moving down the alleyway to the rear of the shop. He mused about the protection on the door latch; it hadn't felt like a Knot but had been some other type of topomantic working. Perhaps an origamantic folding of some sort.

Escher approached the rear door. There was a prosaic sign in the window with the words "Back At:" but instead of the standard single clock face with hands, there were nine clock faces, each showing a time of eight in the morning. There was no visible lock on the door, but the latch lever didn't move. Escher murmured, "I wonder," and moved one of the hands by one hour. The three faces adjacent to that one moved their hands by two hours in the opposite direction.

Escher withdrew the newly-acquired pocket watch and consulted the time. Then he set one of the clocks to the current time. Nothing happened other than scrambling of nearby faces. He started moving the hands of the nine clock faces to build up a map of which set of faces was moved by each hand. Then he started feeling his way towards the sequence that would align all of the faces at the end. He succeeded after fifteen minutes, but by then the time had already passed and the door remained locked. He set a new target time ten minutes in the future and began to work on aligning the dials on the new time. The last clock clicked into place with one minute to spare, then he had to wait another long minute before his watch agreed with the nine faces, and he heard the faint snick of the lock mechanism. He pressed the latch lever once more, and this time the door opened.

Escher entered, trailed by Trefoil. They found themselves in the back room of the shop, where faint lamplight from the street picked out the hulking form of cases and cabinets and the low shadows of workbenches. Tiny glints reflected from movements that rotated slowly in the darkness, measuring out the passing seconds of the night. If vision was nearly useless because of the lack of light, hearing was even worse; all the clocks ticked and whirred and tinkled, filling the shop with ceaseless industry. The smell of metal and oil drifted in the air, adding its own distraction. The only reliable sense remaining was touch, so Escher felt his way carefully through the shop.

Trefoil leaped gracefully onto a workbench, sending a shower of small gears spilling from the bench onto the floor.

"Shh!"

"I meant to do that."

Escher froze as the bouncing gears ahead of him vanished in flashes of blue light. He backed up to the door, careful to only step where he had previously trodden. He groped behind him until he found the broom that he had noted on the way in (for possible use as a weapon or doorjamb in emergencies). He moved slowly forward again, tapping the floor as he went. Just past where Trefoil sat, the broom went through the floor and was almost yanked from his hands. Tapping like a blind man, he mapped out a square three feet on a side where the solid floor was … missing. On his knees, he peered down into the depths and thought he saw far-off stars at the bottom. He risked a match, down near the floor, and dropped it into the square. As it passed the level of the floor, it accelerated into a streak that snuffed out the flame. In that brief second, he saw a pit receding into infinity down a bleak and apparently airless shaft. In the distance were some objects. One of them might have been the figure of a person — perhaps a previous thief.

"Thanks, Trefoil."

"I told you, I meant to do that."

Escher reflected that he might never know the truth of that statement as he climbed up on a bench to sidle past the pit. He checked his footing carefully with the broom handle before climbing down on the other side, and continued to tap his way to the glass cabinet that contained the compass. He ran his hands up and down a few inches from the glass, feeling for further traps. He found none, but the case was locked, and Fourquereau had not been thoughtful enough to leave the key in the lock.

He had lock picks, of course. He knew how to use them in the dark. But when he started to explore the lock before him, he found it was like nothing he had encountered before. The channel corkscrewed tightly inside so that his pick couldn't get past the turns to reach the pins. It must take a very interesting key to operate this lock.

Escher extracted a square of paper from his pocket. Working by touch alone, he folded the paper into a complex construction, reminiscent of the origami of his world, but using some techniques that his teacher had called the Forbidden Folds, which used the art of topomancy in ways similar to the Knots that he usually favored. However, origamancy was the tool that he needed for this task. He inserted the end of the paper figure into the gap between door and frame of the cabinet and worked it deep into the bolt of the lock. Then, when he blew gently on the paper, it expended in place, pushing the bolt back into the lock. The door swung open.

He reached cautiously inside, mindful of potential traps such as the one Molendinarii had sprung on him. Nothing tried to snare, impale, or poison him as he gingerly lifted the compass from its shelf. There was no time to examine it, nor light to see it, so he secured it in a lined pouch and began to retrace his steps.

He had just crossed the bottomless pit when the knob of the back door rattled. He froze, thinking that the proprietor had returned, or worse, a passing member of the night watch had noticed the unlocked door. His only other exit would be through the front door, but he didn't know if it was locked from the inside or how many undiscovered traps lay between him and the street. He could leap the pit easily enough, but the next one would be unknown and likely just as deadly. He turned to face the back door, deciding that the chance of escape that way was higher. He kicked himself for not readying a Knot to confound an attacker.

The knob turned and the door opened cautiously. Perhaps it wasn't the night watch after all; they would be more assertive. The silhouette that stepped inside had a tatty jacket and an ivy cap, hardly standard issue for the watch. Escher released the breath that he was holding; it was just an opportunist finding an unlocked door.

The intruder startled at the sound. "Oy! Who's there?" He hefted a short billy club and squinted into the darkness.

"No one at all. I got what I came for and I'll be on my way. You can have whatever's left."

"So you got the most valuable item? Hand it over and I'll let you out." The intruder blocked the doorway and waited.

Escher ducked behind a workbench and shuffled his shoes to make the sounds of quick running steps. Then he grabbed a small tool and tossed it towards the front of the shop.

"Trying to get out the front? I'll show you." The intruder strode quickly towards the source of the noise, right up to the edge of the pit. After that, the scream went on for a long time, only gradually diminishing with distance.

"Should have taken my first offer," said Escher, slipping out the back door. Trefoil followed. Outside, another figure was moving stealthily down the alleyway. Escher reached for his Knot of Disregard. He had used it earlier, but it still held together — for now. It had become frayed and delicate, but it should get him out of the neighborhood. He activated the Knot and walked calmly past the approaching robber who obligingly took no notice of him. As he neared the next cross street, he heard Fourquereau's door open and close. Seconds later, all the bells in the shop rang frantically. A light went on inside the shop, and he could see the erstwhile robber through the window of the back door, pounding on it to get out. Escher turned onto the wide and deserted street and headed towards the observatory. The Knot of Disregard expired, falling into powder in his pocket, but Escher continued walking unhurriedly. He had a lot of practice in looking uninteresting on his own, without assistance from Knots.

Encounters

The Plurs Chasm

February 28, 2016

Word has reached us here in Plurs that the city and geogon of Berlin has been constructing an apparatus to allow people to communicate over long distances. Called a telewriter, this device sends taps written in a special code via wires strung over the land. To date, these have been used only within a single geogon. The messages must be transcribed, carried across the chasms, and resent on another telewriter system to cross that geogon. Work is progressing on methods for these methods to cross the chasms, which will be a boon to commerce and news across the world.

The following evening, the man named Escher called on Emeline Cigne at her townhouse. He carried the compass in his pocket, planning to present it as a surprise. He had made a reservation for dinner and had sent her an invitation early in the day. She had accepted with gratifying swiftness by return messenger.

A butler answered the door. "Please tell Mlle Cigne that M. Resche has come to call. She is expecting me."

The butler looked impassively at him without moving out of the door. "She informed me that I should expect a M. Escher."

"I ... answer to that name also."

"Will M. Chesrè be joining us as well?"

"Not tonight. Three's a crowd."

The butler stood aside, evidently feeling that he had discharged his duties in intimidating the interloper. Escher was left to wait in a parlor. The interior of Emeline's home was understated and tasteful, with a few fine pieces of art on the wall, carpets on the floor that appeared to be hand-woven, and furniture that thought highly of itself but still did its job comfortably and with a minimum of fuss. Very much like Emeline herself, thought Escher, though at odds with the cyclonic nature of her office. Perhaps she had multiple personas for work life and private. The idea appealed to him.

As he stood in the parlor, Escher fingered the compass in his pocket, wondering when he should give it to Emeline. Should he present it when she walked in or wait until later and build up the suspense? It would be enjoyable to draw out the tension, but on the other hand, it would make a more relaxed evening if he made the reveal at the beginning. As he weighed the scenarios in his mind, he walked around the room fingering the small objects that made small statements of interest or importance. A translation of the Odyssey lay open to the return of the wandering king to Ithaca. The frontispiece of the volume bore the name Piers Cigne in a precise hand. An old coin, mounted for display, might be ancient Roman in origin. A Buddha statue in a niche, a small chime nearby. A small statue of a bull, carved from black, dense wood. A map of the ancient world centered on the Mediterranean. Dragons lurked at the edges.

"These are all things that my uncle Piers brought home from his travels," said Emeline quietly behind him. Escher turned quickly.

"Sorry, you startled me," he said. Recovering, he gestured at the items on display. "He did seem to travel extensively."

"Yes, he always told the best stories."

And the compass belonged here with this collection, thought Escher. He reached into his pocket, ready to produce it with a flourish. However, his hand encountered instead a shape rounded and smooth, with the warmth of wood, not the chill of metal. He had pocketed the statue of the bull. He was momentarily flustered and cast around for an out. "It's been a long time since the world looked like that," he said, indicating the map.

Emeline looked that way. "Yes, I suppose it has."

Escher silently returned the bull to the shelf while her attention was turned away. He decided to present Emeline with the compass later, after his nerves settled. "Shall we head out to dinner?"

"You didn't say what you had in mind."

"I made a reservation at Pla dels Àngels, if that is satisfactory."

"How could it not be?"

It unfolded that this restaurant was a favorite of Emeline's, and with good reason. The food was exquisite and in a completely different style from their previous dining experience. Escher would have called it Catalan-influenced, though the maps of this world identified no such region.

Early in the meal, Escher again reached into his pocket to produce the compass but found that he had stolen a silver spoon from the table, which he returned. At his next attempt, he found the sommelier's engraved corkscrew. It was a very fine corkscrew, and he was certain that worthy would be quite loathe to lose it. As the master of wines glided past again, a furrow between his eyes and obviously scanning for his missing instrument, Escher slipped it into the man's apron pocket. A hushed blasphemy in Spanish a moment later told Escher that it had been discovered.

It felt to Escher that his personas were at war with each other. His outer persona wanted to do the right thing and return the compass to Emeline. His inner self wanted it to examine, to understand, to use on his own behalf. He resolved to give it to her when they returned to her townhouse, along with an explanation of his inner conflict. Surely she would help him.

"Are you still fixed on a course of finding a way home?"

Escher looked at her sideways. "Why would I waver?" he said defensively.

"What do you have in that world that you do not have here?"

"It's more about something that I left unfinished."

"Can you tell me about it?"

"I'd rather not talk about it. It would spoil the mood."

The awkward silence that followed was interrupted by the arrival of the next course. Conversation resumed about the food and other inconsequentials, but for Escher the meal had lost some of its savor.

On their way home, Emeline seemed to be searching for words.

"I'm a nosy person … as I've admitted. I made a career out of it, and it's become a virtue. So I'm not very practiced at admitting when my nosiness goes off target and causes …"

"Shh!"

"Look, I'm trying to say I'm sorry …"

"No, Shh! Footsteps."

The cosh missed Escher's head by an inch only because he had already started to turn. He lashed out and slapped his assailant with the Knot of Confusion that he had ready inside his sleeve. The man staggered away. Another had grabbed Emeline, but she stomped his foot with a shoe that had suddenly grown a knife blade, then flicked an origami paper shape at him. He creased down his center line, turned two-dimensional and folded closed like a book, first vertically, then horizontally, until he disappeared.

The first thug was still at large, flailing at the air near Escher. Escher slapped a second Knot on the other side of a head that had lost a beauty contest with a cauliflower. The thug went down, retching.

"Are you unhurt?" he asked Emeline.

"I'm fine. What did you hit him with?"

"Two Knots of Confusion, one twisted clockwise, one counter-clockwise. It induces severe vertigo."

"You fight dirty."

"Not as dirty as he was prepared to fight." Escher pocketed the cosh and removed a set of brass knuckles from the heavy's left hand. Cauliflower Face looked distressed, then abruptly vomited. He tried to make it count for something, aiming at Escher, but missed.

"Who sent you?" demanded Escher.

"Ain't tellin."

"It was Molendinarii, wasn't it?"

"Who dat?." The smell of rotting teeth made Escher gag. Half were already gone, accounting for his less-than-precise diction.

"Let's jog your memory," said Emeline sweetly, as she tucked another origami figure into the thug's coat. She pulled out an identical figure and opened the first fold. The man's eyes bugged out.

"Now, who sent you?"

"Ungh. Ain't ... tellin."

Emeline held the paper before the man's eyes and very slowly opened another fold. Sweat beaded on his lumpy forehead and he moaned. She slowly began to twist the figure;

he clutched at his stomach with a screech, but still refused to talk. She held the figure in front of his eyes with both thumbs and forefingers positioned on either side of a crease. "Do you want to find out what happens when I tear this?"

"No! He din't tell me I was chasing ta devil!"

"Who?" said Escher and Emeline simultaneously.

"It was just a messenger. I don't know who sent 'im."

"Should I crumple him up?" Emeline held the origami figure in her open fist.

"No, he doesn't know."

Emeline folded her paper once more, and Cauliflower Face creased and disappeared in the manner of his colleague.

"Should we drop these in the river?" asked Emeline.

"Er, no. I have no stomach for that. We can just deposit them in a trash bin and leave it to fate if someone finds it."

"What if a child finds them and unfolds them?"

"That wouldn't do, would it? I guess I'll keep them and drop them at the magistrate's office in the morning."

There were footfalls behind them, measured and heavy. Someone had practiced a menacing gait to perfection. No, at least two someones. Escher and Emeline hurriedly turned down a side street, looking for a way to a safer part of town, one where there were still people abroad who didn't want to do them harm. There was no safety this way; a feeling of dread clenched his stomach. Ahead of them, a shadow detached itself from a lamppost and started towards them. It didn't look like a savior.

"I used everything that I had on the first two," said Emeline. "Do you have anything left?"

"Not unless I can distract them with a display of lock picking skill." The fear reminded him of another dark night in the streets of Geneva, when he had also looked for a way to escape. They were in a street of shops, locked and dark at this hour. He could probably vault onto a roof to elude the pursuers, but Emeline wasn't dressed for vaulting. Even if he was the probable target, he couldn't abandon her. He had been burdened by that concern before, as well. He started trying a few nearby doors in the faint hope that one might be unlocked.

"They're moving in," whispered Emeline.

"Wait, I may see a way out." Escher had seen an item on display in the window of the nearest shop. He shook out another Knot from his pocket and applied it to the door lock.

"They're turning the corner." Emeline's voice was more urgent.

"Almost there."

The lock clicked open; the Knot puffed into ash. That was the last lock he could pick this evening. Escher opened the door and ushered Emeline inside, locking the door behind them.

"What now?" she whispered.

Escher had slumped to the floor, his back to the door, breathing in great gasps of air. His hands shook. At least they had held steady for long enough to pick the lock.

"What is it? Were you hurt?"

"That incident that I told you I didn't want to talk about? I *really* didn't want to re-live it."

"Oh."

Escher snaked one hand into the window display and retrieved an object. He crawled away from the door and behind the counter and waved Emeline to follow. "Keep down," he said. "If we're lucky, they'll think they lost us. I don't want to use this unless I have to."

"What is it?"

"A last resort."

A shadow appeared outside the door. The knob rattled. Two more shadows appeared in the window. The sounds of a pry bar could be heard grating in the door frame.

"No good, they saw us go in." Escher felt his teeth chattering as he spoke. "S-sorry, I keep thinking this will end up like last time."

"How did that end?"

"F-five weeks in the hospital, four years in jail."

"Someone was with you that time, too?"

"Yeah. Pulled the alarm and slipped out the back door."

"Let's not repeat any of that ending."

The door crunched and splintered. It wouldn't hold much longer.

Escher took a deep breath. "We're going to have to appeal to the Lady of the castle. Remember that nothing you see will be as it appears." He set the object he had removed from the window on the counter and took Emeline's hand. "Look deeply into the globe," he instructed.

"It's a snow globe with a castle," she said, with a tone of voice that said she suspected he'd lost his mind.

"No, it's a doorway. Now, take a step."

Hands joined, they stepped towards the globe. Nothing happened.

"Maybe we should look for a back door to the shop," Emeline said, starting to sound urgent.

"No, the last thing we want to do is to be caught in the alleyway."

The sound of splitting wood came from the front door. The thug outside rattled it to see if it was loose yet, but the bolt still held.

"Maybe I need to ring the doorbell," muttered Escher. He inverted the globe and set the snow whirling, then placed it back on the counter. "Let's try again."

"Nothing yet. Are you sure about this?"

"It could be just a snow globe. I hope not." Escher twisted the globe slightly to get a better angle on the castle door. The shop door bowed inward to a new assault.

"One last try. One. Two. Step!" They took a long step, which became longer and colder than it seemed it had any right to be.

The door burst open and three roughly-dressed thugs barged through, only to find an empty shop.

Capture

The Plurs Chasm

June 24, 1912 (from the archives)

A man known for incessant playing of the fife outside his home was stabbed to death today, apparently by a neighbor. The Magistrate has ruled it a suicide.

"Where are we?" asked Emeline, sounding unsettled. A long corridor of stone stretched ahead of them, with doors on either side.

"We're in the castle of the Contessa Hesperia," said Escher.

"Who is that?"

"Someone who kidnapped me last week and tormented me with honey dates."

"What?"

"It's a long story and one that's likely to be misinterpreted. Let's hope we don't meet the Contessa."

"Where do these doors go?"

"Many different places, but none that are going to do us any good. I think we have to go through the center of the castle."

"What's in the center?"

"The spider's lair."

Escher led Emeline down the corridor to the end. An ornate door opened to the left. Escher passed it on tiptoes. "The spider's bedroom," he whispered. "Let's hope she's asleep."

"How do you know where the spider's bedroom is?" whispered Emeline.

If Escher intended to answer, he was cut short by the door at the end of the hallway swinging slowly open. They entered cautiously. Contessa Hesperia was not to be seen, but her voice issued from the air around them. The voice was gnarled and nasal, not the seductive honey of his previous visit. But it was her voice, without a doubt.

"Welcome back, Escher," she said. "For your sake, I do hope you've brought my ruby with you."

Escher shrugged, affecting an outward calm that he didn't feel."I don't carry it about on my person when I go out for a stroll. Unfortunately, a gang of thugs caused us to take a shortcut through a snow globe I happened to find." He was reverting to the persona he had used with her before, which all things considered might be a mistake.

"You removed it from my neck when you departed my bed. Now you bring another young lady into my sitting room. Mlle Cigne, is it not? You should be careful when he attempts to remove your clothes, my dear. He may take more than you bargain for."

Emeline's voice was cold. "I'm sure he didn't take anything you hadn't lost long ago."

Hesperia stepped from behind a hanging that concealed a door. She had the outward appearance that she had before, other than that her gown was blue instead of green and marginally less transparent. However, her features had an unnatural smoothness and lack of detail. To Escher, it seemed like the unsettling almost-realism of a painted mannequin. Her hair turned briefly to grey before settling back to glossy black. Escher decided that she must not have enough power left for a full glamour to cover her physical appearance.

The Contessa picked up a Rubik's Cube from the table and began idly turning it. There were a number of these around in various configurations, some solved, some random, and some twisted artistically. "You should be careful how you speak to a lady in her castle," she said.

"If I see one, I will," retorted Emeline.

Hesperia twisted the cube in her hand — top, left, top, and back again. A cube of space containing Emeline tilted upwards and slid sideways, disappearing from sight as it did so.

"What have you done with her?" cried Escher.

"I grew weary of listening to her sniping, so I put her away for safekeeping. Now, I want that ruby." Hesperia's glamour wavered, and she began to diminish, to darken like old mahogany and to bend and twist to match.

"I'll go get it right now."

"No, I don't think so. I'll keep Mlle Cigne for now. I want you to bring the gem to the old bridge on the north of town tomorrow night, the one they call the Bridge of Souls. I'll bring your little swan with me, and we'll trade there."

"What? Why then? Why there?"

"Because they're the time and place I've chosen, and I think you're not in a position to ask questions. Take the door on your right and go through the third door on your left in the hallway."

Escher stumbled out of the parlor, stunned at the sudden turn the encounter had taken. Outside in the corridor he stopped, wondering if he should give in to the rage that urged him to rush back in and physically overwhelm Hesperia. He held himself in check with the strong suspicion that he would just end up in another cube or some other unseen trap. She held the cards for now.

Escher pushed through the door onto the streets and found himself near the observatory. He bent over, hands on knees, giving himself over to a case of shakes. Emeline was gone. Imprisoned, he hoped, but he had only Hesperia's word for that. He had to hold onto that hope, as bad as it was, because the alternative was worse. Hesperia had to be the one who had sent those thugs to manipulate him into fleeing into the castle. Manipulation made him very, very angry.

He made his way up to the observatory. Trefoil was waiting for him.

"I sense it didn't go well. Did you make a fox paw during dinner?"

"What? No, we were assaulted, went to Hesperia's castle, and Hesperia is holding Emeline hostage."

"I knew I should have gone with you to protect you."

"I have to bring her ruby to the Bridge of Souls tomorrow night. If she harms Emeline I'll kill her! I'll tear her castle apart and smash all her snow globes so she's trapped on her mountainside." He folded down into a seat and put his head in his hands.

He felt paws on his knee. He looked up to find Trefoil stretched up from the floor to look into his face. "We'll get her back," said the cat. "I'll help you."

"Thanks, buddy." Escher scratched him behind the ears. "I'm not sure what you can do, but that's good to know."

"We can watch each other's tails."

"Ah, right. And ... fox paw?"

"Everyone knows that 'false step' makes no sense at all. It got mangled when it was translated into French. A fox paw is much worse."

Escher thought of Hesperia, hidden in her glamour in her castle. "Yes, this definitely was a fox paw."

❖

Escher thought for a while as the lights in the windows of the town winked out below the observatory. After a time, he laid his cloak out on the table and took stock of the content of the many pockets on the inside. He spent a number of hours with lengths of cord after that, crafting some Knots and filling his pockets with them. Some, one in particular, were difficult, time-consuming and complex to prepare. That one in particular took him several hours to prepare to his satisfaction. He regretted that he wouldn't be able to test it, but he didn't have time to prepare another after that one was used. Still unable to sleep, he read some of the stack of the Plurs Chasm that Moonbird had accumulated, but every one of Emeline's bylines that he read sawed at his fears until they were echoing like an out-of-tune violin in his head. Finally, near dawn, he fell asleep from exhaustion and got a few hours of sleep, if not exactly rest.

He arose mid-morning after the bank opened. He went directly there and withdrew a large portion of the funds he had on account. Then he went to the Town Hall and filed a will in which Trefoil would inherit his house on Twopenny Lane, with Emeline as executor because of the likely objections that Trefoil wasn't the right species to own a house. He could think of quite a few humans that were less qualified than his companion. With great reluctance, he added a clause that this responsibility would pass to Emeline's estate if the worst happened. He felt a dread even thinking about it, as if writing it down made it more real. But he wanted to make sure Trefoil was provided for. Once he had the will signed and counter-signed, he filed it and posted a copy to the newspaper office.

Next, he crossed town to the shop of Metrophanes. The jeweler greeted him somewhat cautiously as he walked in the door. "Welcome, good sir. Are you interested in another one of the pieces that you looked at previously?"

Escher recalled with sudden regret that he hadn't given the pendant to Emeline. "Yes, I believe I might be."

"And was your previous gift well-received?"

"Yes, my partner was delighted." Escher noted how easily the lie came to his lips. Perhaps Emeline had a point about his readiness to twist the truth.

"Something more substantial this time, I think. Could I see a few of your rings?"

He pretended to dither over the selection of rings, making the Ring of Perception his third choice because of its expense and shaking his head over the other two that he said weren't quite right. Eventually, he got Metrophanes to come down by nearly twenty-five percent, not because he couldn't afford the ring now that he was liquidating everything but because the reflex to haggle was so deeply ingrained.

Escher next went to the Fractalist temple, where he waited in the entryway. He didn't have time to navigate the maze, and he suspected that Wharnebie had ways of knowing what happened in his temple and beyond. He had waited about twenty minutes when an arrhythmic thumping announced the approach of the priest. When he appeared, Escher asked, "Is the next realignment going to happen tonight?"

Wharnebie looked at him carefully with his steady eye. The wandering eye was more frantically active than before, as if searching for something. "Tonight is the four hundredth anniversary of the Geography Disaster, so some might think it imminent, yes, but my measurements of the strains indicate that sometime in the next week is more likely."

"Hesperia has taken my friend hostage and is demanding that I bring her ruby to the Bridge of Souls tonight. I think they're about to play their Game."

"You have Hesperia's ruby? My, my. You may be right. The potential energy is not at its peak yet, but it is certainly enough for them to trigger the realignment prematurely, yes. They may have calculated their advantage to be greater in other ways at this time, or they hope to move before all the other Players are ready. I thank you for warning me."

"Is there anything you can do?"

"I can tell you not to give Hesperia her ruby."

"I'm afraid I might not have that option."

"I understand. This is your way home."

"That's not what I ... it is?"

"Make your choices carefully and keep your eye on your goal. Your inner eye, that is."

"How do I ... Wait!" But Wharnebie was gone again.

Escher turned back towards the observatory, hoping that he knew what his goal was.

Bridge of Souls

The Plurs Chasm
September 5, 2018

A local police precinct reported yesterday that an unidentified man left two origami figures and various implements of violence on the desk of the sergeant on duty. The sergeant reports that when he unfolded the papers, there emerged two thugs who were well-known and wanted for a series of robberies. The sergeant has been suspended pending investigation of drinking on the job. The police chief was quoted, "Well done and that for putting them away, but, really? Wrapped up in little bits of paper?"

The man named Escher came to the Bridge of Souls at midnight. It was indeed a bridge, and it did cross a chasm, but it wasn't as simple as that. The sides of the chasm were unequal in height, and the bridge accommodated this by twisting to the left, plunging downward, doubling back with a half-twist, rejoining itself, then departing again to land on the far side. Once on the bridge, it appeared to be short and straight, but walking across it took half of forever, and at times the far end drew closer, and at other times it receded. The land on one side was Swiss farmland; the land on the other was a Norwegian forest. This was the chasm where the Geography Disaster had originated. While it was difficult to cross between the scrambled geogons of the earth at any point, this was by far the most treacherous crossing.

There he found Molendinarii. They met in the middle of the bridge. It was hard to discern the middle of such an uncertain geometry, but it was conveniently marked with an engraving of a compass rose. Fog had risen thickly around them, hiding the chasm from view. Escher fingered the Ring of Perception in his pocket. He had expected distortions and illusions in the chasm, and had armed himself with the Ring as a way to combat them. He had to hold it for the moment of greatest need, otherwise it might well be too hot to hold when it would do him the most good.

Molendinarii was occupied with some task when Escher approached. He looked up and snarled, "What are you doing here?"

"Contessa Hesperia requested my presence."

Molendinarii's expression was interesting. Annoyance, anger, and possibly … pity? What was behind Hesperia's demand? He nodded at the space behind Escher.

Contessa Hesperia stepped onto the bridge. She was cloaked but seemed somewhat diminished within its folds. A wisp of graying hair escaped her hood. "My ruby, boy?"

"You have the cube?"

Hesperia extended the cube in a hand that was aged and hardening into a claw. Escher held out a pouch containing the ruby; they exchanged. Hesperia immediately put it on. Her form straightened and filled out her robe again.

Three additional figures stepped onto the bridge from the south. As they approached, Escher asked conversationally, "I've been wondering how this bridge got its name. Could you enlighten me?" As he did so, he began solving the cube by touch, with only a glance to memorize the colors.

"The Bridge of Souls?" said Molendinarii. "Many people end their life here." His animosity appeared to have been put on hold by Hesperia's intervention.

"I suppose it is an attractive place to go if you want to … go."

"People seldom come with that intent. The geometry simply drives them mad."

The hooded figures had drawn up around them. Escher completed the final twist on the cube. Emeline stumbled out into the middle of the circle. She was still wearing the dress and cloak from the evening before. She looked about in bewilderment.

"What am I doing here? Who are these people?"

"You have been stuck in Hesperia's cube since last evening. I just freed you in exchange for her ruby. We're in the middle of the next great Game, and these are the Players." He reached into his pocket and pulled out the compass, under cover of his cloak. "Here. Do you know how to use this?"

"I think so."

"Are the Players all assembled?" asked Molendinarii. There was a ritual feel to his question. Those assembled in the circle lowered their cowls. The twisted walk of the first figure revealed it to be Wharnebie even before he pulled back his hood. The second revealed a face that was unfamiliar to Escher, but the harp he held in his hand said this must be Tanylive, the Apothecary. The third face …

"Who is this?" demanded Molendinarii.

"I could not master the harp in the time I had," said Tanylive. "The Meisterin had a student who has practiced it for years. I have had her memorize the sequences we will need. It is better this way."

The young face was filled with apprehension as she looked at the grim countenances that surrounded her. Her gaze skipped and came back as it passed Escher. "M. Chesrè," she whispered. "I am happy to see your face. I was worried."

Escher hoped her trust wasn't misplaced. "Just go along with it, Mia. I'm sure it will be fine."

Molendinarii peremptorily waved them to silence. "The geomantic strains have built to historic levels in recent days," he told the group. "We have the opportunity for an alignment of unprecedented strength."

"I repeat my warning that this is an irresponsible use of power," said Wharnebie. "We should be making harmonious adjustments to restore the original order of the world, not disarrange it for our benefit."

"It is decided," said Molendinarii dismissively.

"I will oppose."

Molendinarii smiled thinly. "That's why it's a Game." He planted a staff in the center of the compass rose, then placed the glowing Knot in a carved niche in the staff. "I set the center, I establish the direction," he intoned.

"Do you know what is going on?" whispered Emeline.

"They're inducing, or at least directing, the next geomantic realignment. It sounds like a major one."

"Is this your way home?"

"I'm sure this is how I got here at least. Getting home is more complex than I anticipated. I thought I could just open the doorway with the right artifacts, but there's more to it."

Hesperia stood on the west edge of the circle. She removed her ruby once more and tossed it to the south. It orbited those standing in the circle, rising higher to the north, lower to the south. "I establish the perimeter, the plane, and the chord."

Molendinarii paused and surveyed the circle. "Have all Players declared themselves?"

Emeline stood straight. "As the heir of Piers Cigne, I will take his place." Escher's jaw dropped. He should have guessed Piers was a Player, but that Emeline knew this was a surprise.

"What do you bring to the Game? Being the heir of a former Player is not enough."

"I bring his compass. Indeed, I don't know how you expected to succeed without it."

Molendinarii looked vexed but conceded with a wave. Hesperia opened her mouth to object, but Molendinarii cut her off, saying, "She's right. Now that all Players have declared themselves …"

"There's one more."

Everyone other than Escher looked around. He didn't need to. This was typically brash; he should have expected it. He wanted to roll his eyes but kept his face impassive.

"Who speaks? Show yourself."

"I'm right here, Lord Doofus. Not there, down here. Do I need to bite your ankle?"

"A cat?"

"Your powers of observation are profound."

"What do you bring to the Game?"

"My mother was the Queen of Siam before it was annexed by Greenland in the Geography Disaster. My father was a prince of Egypt, a direct descendant of the goddess Bastet herself. I was born in the Alley of the Bookbinders in a nest made of shredded topology textbooks. I don't need any artifacts; I *am* magic."

Escher thought that he saw Molendinarii's eye twitching. "And what role do you propose?"

"The same role as I've been playing. If your powers of perception are as great as you believe, you should know what that is."

"Very well, cat. Interfere with us at your own peril. We cannot delay any longer. Harpist, commence."

Tanylive handed the harp to Mia, who took up the two small mallets and struck the strings once. The note quivered in the misty air for a long moment before she eased into a meandering melody that lead the ear as a mandala leads the eye. Without trying, Escher fell into a trance in which he followed the music through cascades of notes, first gradually focusing on a single melody line, then opening out into an expansive theme that suggested that the entire universe could be encapsulated in a single crystalline moment.

Wharnebie held up the Cosmic Mandala with a bell suspended beneath it. He struck the bell and began droning a low atonal chant. It had its own rhythm, which demanded the attention of the listeners. The harp notes took on a harsh note in comparison, occasionally dropping out altogether, though whether that occurred for the player or the listener was difficult to say. The notes of the harp had been a promise, which was now diminished. Mia frowned and tried to compensate

Molendinarii was drawing symbols of light in the air with a wand. He wrote unfamiliar terms in matrices that had width and breadth and depth and perhaps dimensions unseen; he set up expressions describing their equivalencies and their inequalities. As he worked, he bound those terms to the notes flowing from the harp until the notes and the terms became one, resonating in sight and sound. The promise of the harp strengthened once again to overwhelm Wharnebie's chanting. The boundaries of the bridge grew indistinct, or perhaps a better word would be indeterminate. It wasn't that they were neither here nor there, but that they were both here and there and at many other points. Escher was reminded of a quantum function, which had an entire set of possible outcomes that would not be determined until the final state was observed.

Now Hesperia stepped up to add a few terms of her own to the matrix. Molendinarii had left the matrix sparse, with terms missing here and there. Hesperia filled these in, though in one instance she appeared to stumble. Escher saw her hand snake out to smudge an existing term, erasing a line that had been there before. It was artfully done, and Molendinarii seemed not to have noticed the alteration.

Emeline stepped forward. "It's my turn to play."

Molendinarii gestured impatiently. "It's not yet time for the compass. Declare your intentions."

"What are you doing?" whispered Escher.

Emeline put the compass in her pocket.

"My play is Escher."

The Great Game

Emeline led the man named Escher to the center of the bridge. "What are you doing?" he repeated.

"Playing the Game. If you want to go home, this is the only way."

"But ..."

"No talking. Stand here."

Emeline turned to the assembled Players. "By the principle of Affinity, this person shall be attracted to the place he originated. The transfer of mass between the worlds will be converted into geomantic energy, which will amplify the amount of realignment available to you. The outcome you seek will be more certain and more far-reaching."

Molendinarii drew a new matrix in the air in glowing symbols, this one at ninety degrees to the previous three. He wrote new analog logic equations relating this new matrix to the others. "This matrix is singular," he said. "We will not be able to invert it."

Hesperia answered, "We may not need to invert it. The presence of Mlle Cigne's 'piece' will provide a determinant for the other terms. This is a solution we have not tried before."

Mia had been in a holding pattern with the music while the unexpected play was made by Emeline. Now she resumed her musical tessellation with a repeating line that gradually evolved greater and greater complexity on every repetition. Molendinarii continued constructing his analogies. Escher now could see that he was building a description of the ways in which another world differed from this one. He used analogies, but not the intuitive "this is like that" of everyday language, but similarity coefficients: a precise formulation of how much like "this" a particular "that" was and the quantifiable differences between them.

Emeline brought the compass to her eye, sighting through the miniature sextant. A star-like point appeared in the foggy darkness above them. Normally, this instrument would measure the altitude and azimuth of a star. But this point was not a star and this instrument wasn't representative of its kind. Emeline moved an adjustment on the compass dial; in response, the entire bridge began to realign itself under their feet. It both rotated around its center and twisted on its axis, while the guide star remained constant.

Wharnebie responded by uncovering a glowing orb that projected a six-sided star on the fog above. The sides segmented and folded, then repeated, then again, and again. As the fractal kept dividing, it rotated segments through the third dimension, but Escher could see that there were more rotations upward toward the north and downward to the south. The position of the guide star above shifted subtly to the north. At first, Escher thought that none of the others had noticed, but then Emeline made an adjustment to the compass to compensate. Escher began to worry. Was that the right response? Was Wharnebie trying to prevent him from returning to his world? What role was Hesperia playing?

It was time to employ the Ring of Perception. He hefted the warm gold in his hand for a moment before sliding it on his finger. As he did so, the fog seemed less obscuring and details became sharper.

Now he could see that Wharnebie's fractal was partially illusion. It wasn't affecting the position of the guide star; it was causing Emeline to over-compensate her adjustments to the compass and move it herself. Escher had to do something about Wharnebie before the priest derailed the process.

Hesperia reached the same decision. She reached within her cloak and withdrew a puzzle of interlocking steel rods. The hand that grasped this object had become gnarled and claw-like; the confrontation was drawing her attention away from maintaining her glamour, or perhaps the Ring of Perception allowed Escher to see through it. She withdrew one rod from its nest and with a flick of her wrist hurled it across the circle to embed itself in Wharnebie's globe. Hesperia dropped the steel puzzle, deliberately and forcefully; with the lock pin removed, the shape disintegrated into a cacophony of bouncing rods that skittered across the paving stones. Wharnebie's globe fell apart as if it, too, had smashed on the stones; shards of light scattered over the bridge. The fractal pattern on the fog above rained down upon them in a sleet of geometric fragments. Wharnebie growled in frustration.

The fog became brittle. Lines appeared in the grayness, first few and coarse, then more and more, finer and finer, until they were surrounded by granular fog, something that resembled sand more than fog. The sandfog began to rotate about the axis of the bridge, bulging out both fore and aft. It didn't swirl the way that fog would. It rolled and tumbled as grains of sand would. Escher felt he was looking down the slope of a giant ant-lion's den.

Hesperia gestured to her ruby, which was still maintaining a protective orbit around their circle. The orbit lengthened into an ellipse, reaching out towards the two ends of the tunnel of sandfog. Like a comet, it retuned at steadily increasing intervals, receding farther into the distance ahead and behind, until with a final gesture, the ruby broke free and sailed forward, untethered. A bright light broke through the sandfog ahead as the ruby pierced the veil. Against the grayness of the sandfog and the red glow of the ruby, this was far brighter, and whiter than either. A ray of daylight shone down the bridge, even though the hour was after midnight.

Emeline stepped forward and placed her hand on Escher's shoulder. "It's my move," she said, then lower, so only Escher could hear, "Walk forward, towards that light. Your home is there. If you look back once, I'll know you felt something. If you look back twice, I'll believe that you aren't certain this is the right choice. If you look back three times ... well, you're good at completing a series."

Escher squeezed her hand in acknowledgment and started walking. The light grew nearer and the sandfog grew closer around him. Should he look back? How did he feel about Emeline? Interested? Wary? Distrustful? All of those and more. From the first, she had her own agenda, her own tricks. She had slipped him a Ring of Truth and then apologized. She had helped him, she had misled him. Was there a mathematical series that weighted all the factors of trust and betrayal and desires — multiple desires with different signs — and past relationships and personality flaws? An equation that could be solved to tell him the right course to take?

There wasn't. But he turned and raised a hand in farewell anyway.

He first saw Emeline, with a tight expression on her face that relaxed into wistfulness as he looked back. He had confirmed something for her. He hadn't needed to; he was never going to see her again, but he had looked back, without consciously deciding that he wanted to. In that moment he knew he had confirmed something for himself as well.

Everyone else's eyes were on him as well, which is why none of them saw Hesperia reach out and erase a symbol in Molendinarii's equations of analogies.

Escher turned to hasten forward. Hesperia was trying to turn the Game to her advantage. He had to hurry while the portal was still open.

The sandfog curled over the edges of the bridge and lapped against his feet. Overhead, the gray substance churned and glinted in the light from the portal. Wisps of blue sky could be seen beyond, along with vague, out-of-focus shapes that might be trees or buildings or maybe even mountains. The sandfog rose over the tops of his feet. Now he could feel the drag and grit of the stuff. It sucked his feet down and made them hard to lift; it pulled him to the right as it swept across the surface of the bridge; and it pushed him forward toward the portal at ever-faster speeds, like sand draining through the neck of an hourglass.

He didn't mean to look behind him a second time, but he did. Did that mean he wasn't certain about this course? All he had wanted for the past year was to go back to his world and resume his life. Could Emeline read him that well, or was he putting too much weight on her words? How could she know how he felt?

But this time when he looked back, Hesperia was facing away from him, arms upraised. A glow was beginning at the opposite end of the spinning tunnel of sandfog. Hesperia wasn't opposing what Emeline or the others were doing; she was using their work for her own scenario in their Game.

The sandfog pulled at Escher's shoes, impelling him forward. He had to look away from the scene behind him to keep his balance. The ring that delimited the plane of contact between this world and his own rushed towards him, swelling as he neared. Now he could see buildings ahead of him, the streets of old-town Geneva where he had made his home.

He surprised himself by turning a third time, just before he reached the portal. He cursed. He knew he wanted to go home; why was his mind tormenting him with this indecision?

The curse died on his lips. A new portal had formed at the far end of the bridge, a new circle of brightness. Something was coming through from that world, just as he was leaving. A towering figure, bright against the sandfog. It ducked its head to clear the portal then stood tall on the far end. The stones of the bridge smoked.

The paintings of hell-creatures on Hesperia's walls hadn't been works of imagination alone. A fire demon, horned, hoofed, and eight feet tall, strode towards the Players on the bridge.

Battle

The man named Escher started to run.

He ran towards the group of Players, away from the portal to his home, where he had a different name. It wasn't calculation that chose his path, it was something he was reluctant to name. He ran. The sandfog pulled at his feet, sucking them down, dragging them away from his goal. It had been enough of a chore to stay upright when he was trying to walk with the current; it was nearly impossible now to run upstream. He knew that if he fell once, the current would sweep him back through the portal, out into his homeworld, before he ever regained his feet.

He fished in the small pockets he had sewn inside his jacket, where he organized his Knots. Confusion, Constriction, Veracity, Disregard, Heat, Captivity. None of these could help him now. There was one other, but the cost was too high. He could only rely on his own strength. He put one foot forward, then another. It felt like running in a nightmare with a monster closing in behind, running as fast as possible and making the progress of a snail. This wasn't a dream; he was running *towards* his monster.

Looking ahead, he saw that the Players were still watching him, unaware of the incursion orchestrated by Hesperia. "Look behind you!" He waved his hands urgently, then pointed. "Something is coming through!"

Several of the Players looked behind them. Molendinarii frowned at Hesperia, but none of them appeared alarmed. Emeline called back, "What are you talking about?"

'There's a fire demon!"

"Where?"

Escher realized they couldn't see it. But why could he? He redoubled his efforts against the sandfog, gradually closing the distance to the group. The demon walked inexorably towards the group from the other side, also struggling against the streaming fog. He suddenly knew that he had been intended as the counter-balance that would allow that creature to come into this world, and now that he had reversed course, both he and the demon fought an uphill battle against each other to make their way fully back into the world. But why couldn't the other Players see that?

His eyes fell on the golden band on his finger. The Ring of Perception was what allowed him to see the demon. He wrenched it from his finger and pitched it to Emeline. "Put this on! Then look behind you!"

Emeline caught the ring in midair and slipped it on her finger. The gasp as she turned to look at the demon's portal told Escher that he had been successful. But he could still see the demon as well; apparently, once you perceived it, the cloaking spell no longer worked on you. "Touch everyone else with the ring!" he called.

Emeline touched Molendinarii's hand. His eyes widened and he cried out in anger. "Hesperia! I warned you not to try this!"

An idea nudged Escher. He pulled out a Knot and pulled at one loop until it stretched long enough to reach the ground, tightening the crossings into an unpickable bundle. He dangled the end of the loop in the sandfog and held the top end in his hand. Almost immediately, he felt a searing cold in his palm. He adjusted his grip so the tip of the cord dangled from his grasp, but still a cold crushed his bones and stung his skin. He gritted his teeth and hoped that the sandfog still had enough moisture in it. The condensation that dripped on his hand to freeze in glittering droplets he took as a good sign.

His boots were getting uncomfortably warm. His feet felt like roasting potatoes inside. Between his feet and his hands, Mark Twain would have said that on the average he felt comfortable. Escher agreed with Twain on statistics; it was too much like lying with math.

The sandfog reached critical temperature and flashed into steam, blasting a clear space around his feet. Free of the drag of sandfog, Escher put on a burst of speed and closed the distance to the group of Players. "This isn't good, right?" he said, coming up beside Emeline.

"Not good at all," said Emeline.

"I knew this would happen," said Wharnebie. "I warned you all."

Molendinarii was trying to repair the damage to his equations, but it was too late. The demon had already crossed the threshold. Mia had stopped playing. Emeline was staring at the compass in dismay. "It doesn't work," she said. "It's not giving any answers."

"You're asking the wrong questions," said Escher.

Emeline sighted through the sextant at the guide star, then looked down at the compass face. Slowly she turned until the needle lined up with the guide reticle. She paled. The needle was pointing directly at Escher.

"The compass says that you're the only one who can stop it," she said. "But it doesn't say whether you will survive it. You can still make it through the portal to your world if you run now. This isn't your fight."

"Yes, it is. I'm counter-balancing the demon. If I run now, it will grow stronger and overwhelm you."

"Hesperia, stop!" The cry came from Wharnebie. Hesperia had walked to stand before the demon, then turned to face the rest.

"This is my last Game," she said. "I've been playing for decades; I don't have enough magic left to last until the next one. I thought I succeeded the last time when I briefly regained my youth, but it faded. This time, with Escher as counterweight, I finally broke through to the higher dimension. This is a being of almost pure magic. It will make me immortal."

The demon took another step forward. Hesperia's cloak burst into flames that rose and mixed with those of the demon. Greasy black smoke billowed into the air, lofting fragments of cloth and ember. In moments, Hesperia stood naked, shriveled, flesh hanging loosely from stick-like arms, but unharmed by the flames. The demon reached down to embrace her, almost tenderly. Now her skin charred and her hair caught fire. Both woman and demon threw their heads back in a primal scream. A flare of light blinded the onlookers.

When the light diminished and eyes were uncovered, it was done. Hesperia and the demon were one. She stood eight feet tall, black as night with red flames flickering over her body. She had filled out, once again smooth and supple, breasts firm, muscles rippling. She laughed, an earthquake that shook stones, jarred bones, and set softer anatomy to quivering. "Oh, it has been so long since I was young! And to have the stature of a demon lord! I am going to have such fun, watching you all compete for the favor of serving me. Please me and life will be good. I'm sure I don't have to draw the corollary."

Molendinarii slashed his wand through the matrix, obliterating the terms that Hesperia had drawn in. A gale of sandfog blasted the bridge, wild sandfog, not evenly streaming as before. The Players were buffeted and torn but Hesperia only laughed at the chaos. Tanylive took advantage of the confusion to produce a knife from his sleeve and hurl it at the demon Hesperia. It was a good knife and a good throw that flew true at her heart. With the gesture of a flaming hand, the knife reversed course and became a thousand knives that left the air breathless with their passage. They were good knives, and returned as true as the one that was thrown. There was little left of Tanylive beyond some bloody shreds.

Mia stood from where she had sheltered from the knife storm. "M. Chesrè, is that an *ifrit*?"

Escher didn't consider himself an expert on demon species. "Close enough."

"Then I will help." She moved some bridges on the harp to change the tuning, then picked up her mallets and began hammering out a plangent melody. The demon began to twitch, and then to dance.

Wharnebie began an attack with interlocking rings that appeared intended to bind the demon with shackles. Hesperia shrieked with rage and fought to get her limbs under control. Escher thought both attacks were useful distractions but didn't really stand a chance against a creature this strong. He turned to Emeline. "Use your compass," he said, holding open his jacket to reveal the pockets within. "Choose the ones that will work the best."

Emeline held the compass up and immediately pointed to one pocket. It was the same one he had decided against using moments ago. Escher groaned. "It had to be that one. It only works for five seconds and I'll be helpless afterward."

Emeline continued and picked out a second one, then veered and pointed to one that he wore on his wrist. "That one? Are you sure?"

"Yes, it's very strong."

Escher turned back to the battle. Wharnebie was bound in his own shackles now; Escher had missed how that had happened. Mia continued playing, but Hesperia was regaining control of her body. Molendinarii was constructing a new matrix but seemed far from finishing. "Wait!" Emeline called. Escher turned his head; Emeline placed a hurried kiss on his lips. "For luck."

As Escher started to advance, Trefoil leaped in front of him, facing Hesperia. "Trefoil! Get back! She'll make pâté out of you."

Trefoil only twitched his tail, staring daggers at Hesperia. He took a single step towards the demon, then a second. One deliberate step at a time, he advanced, his eyes locked on Hesperia's. The demon took a step backward, looking to both sides. Her foot wobbled as the harp tried to bind her movements to its notes once more. Trefoil's confidence shook her; he was an unknown quantity and he had declared his magical pedigree. "Stay back, cat!" she warned.

Trefoil continued his slow advance. Hesperia backed up one more step, but the back of her legs hit the side of the bridge. "Call off your cat, Escher!"

"The cat does what he wants," said Escher, slipping the first Knot over his wrist. This was the Knot with a cost, the Knot of Time. The moments stretched out in front of him, infinite new moments opening up between those experienced by anyone not wearing the Knot. Escher stepped through those moments while everyone else took the long way around. A blast of fire left Hesperia's hand and traveled glacially to where Trefoil had been standing. Trefoil wasn't there; he was three feet to the right, still advancing. Escher was passing him now, as another fireball started to form in Hesperia's hands. Still aiming at Trefoil; she hadn't reacted to him yet.

Escher took another stride, in slow motion. One and three-quarters of a second had passed. The fireball was on its way towards Trefoil; Escher felt its heat as it flew by. It was going to miss by a wide margin; Mia had disrupted the demon's aim. Another stride, and another. Hesperia's eyes were turning toward him now, her hand began to rise. He came down on his left foot, rolled to his toes, launched again, right foot extended. He reached for the next Knot. Three seconds had passed.

He threw the Knot of Confusion in the demon's face. He could see it bursting into slow flames as it touched her skin. The effect would be short-lived, only until the Knot was consumed. She staggered; Escher hoped it would be enough. He threw the third Knot at her feet.

This was the Knot of Heat that he had used before on the sandfog. One end of the Knot wrapped around Hesperia's leg and the other one landed on the bridge.

All of Hesperia's demon heat grounded itself through the Knot. Stone glowed white and slumped. A section of the railing vanished. Hesperia teetered on the edge of a sudden semi-circle of open air that dropped away underneath her. Her mouth was open in a dopplered scream of rage, as a bundle of fur and claws hit her in the chest.

Hesperia and Trefoil dropped through the hole into the void.

Home

With the last fraction of a second left to him, Escher threw himself over the edge of the bridge, hanging on with one hand, reaching with the other one, trying to avoid the still-glowing edges of the melted stone. Then his five seconds were up. The world became a blur.

He was lying on the ground, the Players standing around him. He took a breath that he had been holding for ten minutes.

"He's moving again, yes," observed Wharnebie.

"Let me see." Emeline elbowed her way past and knelt down beside Escher. She reached out to touch his hands where they lay crossed over his chest. When had they gotten placed like that?

"What happened to you?" Emeline asked.

His chest hurt as he drew a breath. "The compass chose a Knot of Time for me. It has a cost. No one gets extra time; the Knot only compresses ten minutes worth of time into five seconds. Once the five seconds are up, the user is frozen until the rest of the world catches up with the time that he has used. Where's Hesperia?"

Molendinarii answered. "The bridge was between worlds when she went over the side. She'll fall forever through the void between until she dies of hunger. With the demon powers that she absorbed, she'll probably last ten thousand years or more."

Escher shivered to contemplate that fate. Then the last seconds of the fight came back to him. "Trefoil! He sacrificed himself. He went over too."

"You won't get rid of me that easily," said a familiar voice.

"Trefoil! How? I thought you were gone!"

"You caught me by the tail at the last second. I *should* scold you for grabbing my tail like that, but I'm feeling generous right now. Then I scrambled back up. Oh, er, sorry for the damage."

Escher became aware that his sleeve was shredded and several deep gouges marked his arm.

"Don't worry about it. It's a price I'm willing to pay."

"I didn't say I was worried about it. It just seemed good form to say I was sorry." Trefoil groomed his shoulder nervously, and Escher knew he was only blustering.

Escher struggled to his feet. Emeline helped awkwardly, switching sides so she could hold his undamaged arm for support.

"We owe you a great debt," said Molendinarii. When Escher thought the night could hold no more surprises, the note of respect in Molendinarii's voice proved him wrong. "There may still be time to re-open the portal to your world while the fabrics are already weakened. You can still go home if you wish."

Escher looked at Emeline. He thought he caught an edge of wistfulness before she hid it. Did she want him to stay or to go? He looked at Trefoil, then at the rest. They knew him as a thief. Did they want to get rid of him?

Emeline reached up. She slid the Ring of Perception on the finger of his undamaged hand.

All did not become clear. The Ring made the obscure more apparent; it did not make it any less complicated. But it was enough. He knew that one betrayal, five years in the past, didn't mean he should never put his trust in another again. "No, thanks," he said. "I think I'll stay."

The look on Emeline's face told him that he was making a wise choice. For a change.

❖

First light was pushing blue fingers into the sky as the party made their way back into the outskirts of town. Without Hesperia and Tanylive, five people and one cat traveled the road together, not necessarily because they were eager for more of each other's company, but because there was only one road back.

Molendinarii looked at Mia speculatively. "Where did you learn to make demons dance?"

"It was part of my training. If you suspect someone of being possessed by an *ifrit*, play that melody for them. If they dance, they are possessed. A master harpist can drive the *ifrit* out by making it dance to exhaustion, but only if the possessed person is strong enough to endure the dance."

"I doubt that would have worked in this case, with a demon that strong, but at least you distracted her and spoiled her aim."

Mia gave him a shy smile.

Molendinarii left their company first, on the side road that lead to his castle on the hill outside town. In the morning light, he was older and more lined, and quite a bit less fierce looking, than he had been before. Hesperia had not been the only one using a glamour to enhance her image. Molendinarii turned to Escher and raised his hand. "I will consider our score cleared, as long as you never attempt to steal from me again."

"I've had my fill of thievery. However, we still have the matter of the murder of Lady Moonbird between us."

"What! You murdered Lady Moonbird?"

Escher was taken aback. "No, you did. For telling me about your Knot."

"Moonbird was a dear friend. I would never harm her. Someone must answer for this!"

Emeline opened her compass and murmured to it. "Is Lady Moonbird's killer among us?"

The needle swung erratically for a moment, then pointed in the direction of Molendinarii, who began to turn purple with rage. Emeline held up a hand and took a step to the side. The needle didn't waver, but it was no longer pointing at Molendinarii; it was pointing back toward the Bridge of Souls.

Wharnebie said, "Hesperia did it. She was always sowing divisions between the Players. She wanted to take out a Player and make it look like Molendinarii did it. She's also the one who suggested Tanylive as a replacement."

Escher turned back toward Molendinarii. "Perhaps we can begin again?"

Molendinarii's eyes narrowed. "I offered gratitude, not friendship. Do not mistake one for the other." He turned and made his way up the path to his home.

The next to depart was Wharnebie, who stopped at a roadside shrine. "I wish to meditate here for a time," he said. "My offer still stands. You could become an initiate in our temple and seek the answers to your mysteries in a different way."

"Thank you, but I don't think I'm cut out for contemplation."

"I know. You take action. That's why we're all still here this morning, yes? Tomorrow, who knows?" Wharnebie entered the shrine. Escher peered inside a moment later, but the chamber was empty.

They entered the town. Mia took her leave as they passed near the Daughters of the Road. "I wish to tell my sisters that we can do even more than they told us. I will tell them how I made a demon dance."

Near the town center, one of the cafes was just opening for breakfast. Escher and Emeline sat in the open-air seating, ordered tea and croissants, and watched the morning mists evaporating above the rooftops.

"What made you think you were prepared to be a Player?" ask Escher.

"I thought two unprepared people might have a better chance than one."

"Two unprepared people and a magical cat," said another voice.

"Oh, hello, Trefoil. Where have you been? We saved some cream for you."

"Cats never say where they've been."

"You said your role in the Game was the same as it always had been. What was that?"

"Protecting my meal ticket, of course. And bluffing."

The two humans laughed. The cat, of course, did not.

Emeline returned her attention to Escher. "Your turn. Why did you change your mind about going home?"

"Ah, well. First, I did a scrying where I asked where I might find happiness. I was disappointed that it pointed to the bridge and not to you. I think now that meant that we both had to go to the bridge to find that particular destiny. Then I put on the Ring of Perception during the Game. With it I could see clearly there was no real reason to go home and some excellent reasons to stay."

"I see. Anything else?"

Escher reached out to hold Emeline's hand. "Yes, I could see very clearly I was giving up someone of great worth, just because another person a long time ago made me afraid to trust again."

Emeline dimpled. They sat looking into each other's eyes for a long moment, until Trefoil made an impatient sound, and said, "You know, there a nice alley over there if you two want to f—"

"Trefoil!"

"If that's what Escher wants," said Emeline, "he should take me home."

Escher began fiddling with a cord, folding it into an intricate Knot. This was a difficult configuration, but much geomantic energy had been released in the night and the morning was auspicious. He bound the ends together, filled an empty teacup with steaming water from the kettle, and dropped the Knot into the cup. He hadn't answered Emeline yet.

"He's often like this, you know," said Trefoil.

"I know," said Emeline indulgently.

The steam above the cup thickened, then blew outwards in all directions with an explosive puff that rolled across the table and off the edge. The water in the cup cleared, revealing a luminous blue radiance that fell into infinity. "This is like a scrying," he said, "but much harder. This is a foretelling. Something that might happen, perhaps even likely, but not foreordained. It's never worked for me before," he confided.

Emeline looked down into the blue depths. Escher watched bemusement, understanding, and amusement cross her face, intermixed perhaps with something else. She looked up. "This *might* happen?"

Escher bent forward to look into the cup. Far down a blue well, two old people sat in a lush garden on a stone bench.

They were holding hands. As he focused on the scene, he knew those faces. His, and Emeline's, lined with years. Those lines spoke of times that had more often been good than bad.

"It might, with some work." He stood up and held out his hand. "We should get started."

Notes

I hope you've enjoyed this story. Please stop and leave a review on Amazon, Goodreads, or other services that you frequent. Reviews help independent authors reach new readers, such as you.

I would like to thank those who helped make this book possible. My early readers, Dan Elswit and Bob Flynn, who provided feedback and encouragement. My editor, Remy Solomon, who made me take it apart and put it back together in a different order. Rob Scharein, whose web site knotplot.com has a great tutorial on knot theory and many beautiful knots made with his KnotPlot software. Rob graciously gave permission for the use of one of his knot images for the cover of this book. And thank you to the fans of our first book, Sellenria, which encouraged me to keep writing.

If you haven't read Sellenria yet, it's the story of how archaeologist Stenn Gremm sets off to discover the fate of his ancestor, Jonan Gremm, who disappeared on an interstellar voyage four hundred years in the past. Stenn finds a marvelous world where technology no longer works, but something that seems to be magic has power. Stenn learns sword fighting and court intrigue from his guide Gilwyr, ancient lore from the Kir Leth, but strength and purpose he must find within himself. You'll find an excerpt from the novel following this story.

In Sellenria II, coming soon, Jonan Gremm's story is told. How did Jonan come to be stranded on Sellenria, and how did he become associated with The Grimmerroth, the powerful warlock who was at the heart of the great war? Stenn heard the legends, four hundred years later, but legends have a way of distorting the truth.

In Sellenria III, Gilwyr's story, we will learn what happens when the next starship arrives at Sellenria, from which no ship has yet returned. Stenn and Gilwyr must prevent the destruction of the new ship, and Gilwyr struggles with her joint Human-Kir Leth heritage – and her death.

Please visit the website of Lampworks Publishing at https://lamp.works, where you can find newsletters, book reviews, and blogs about books, worldbuilding, and inspirations.

Excerpt from Sellenria

Please enjoy this excerpt from Sellenria: The Starship and the Citadel. Interested? The entire tale
can be found on Amazon, either for your Kindle or
in paperback.

https://www.amazon.com/dp/B07DVWBFXQ

"Before them came Milhadron, before whom there was nothing." Gilwyr was clearly reciting a well-known legend. "Milhadron wished for a place to abide, so he swept out the Ocean
of Light with his hands. On the edge of the Ocean of Light, on
the thin shore against the Mountains of Darkness, he built a
small house, and there he abided.

"Milhadron desired a child so that he could watch the
delight of young eyes seeing everything for the first time. He
created Polnedra to be eternally a child who could play by the
shore of the Ocean of Light. He watched, with the indulgence
that became the trademark of any father who came after, as his
daughter built castles in the sand, tossed stones across the
waters, and made shapes to float over the waves. And the
sandcastles stood as the great towers of stars in our heavens,
and the skipping stones became the planets and the comets
crossing the skies, and the vessels that floated in the Ocean of
Light became our worlds.

"And because Polnedra was created to always delight in
new things, she kept creating, ever smaller and more detailed
creations. She pushed up mountains on her worlds in imitation of the Mountains of Darkness. She poured water where
she had scooped out the mountains and filled the oceans, in
imitation of the Ocean of Light. She made trees to cover the
hillsides. She created smaller creatures to hide among the
trees, and larger creatures to roam the plains. She experiment-
ed; some creatures she made to eat the plants, and some crea-

tures she made to eat each other. Being both a god and a child, she did not yet know of cruelty or kindness.

"She gave to some animals the power of color-shifting because it made more interesting the game between hunter and prey. And from others she withheld it, to see how they would counter that disadvantage. She gave to some creatures, like that ongar that told us about the inn, the power of speech so that she could listen to their chatter. But this came to little more than boasts and threats, and Polnedra quickly bored of it.

"So Polnedra made the first people. She gave to them the gift of speech, as well as something new: the power of thought. These were fine and interesting things, but something was lacking. So Polnedra struck sparks from her hands and let these settle among the people. Each spark contained the tiniest fraction of Polnedra's creativity. Because she left the distribution to chance, the people received greater or lesser sparks, or sometimes none at all. And she watched, and listened, and was amused."

Gilwyr paused, rummaged in her pack for a moment and pulled out what appeared to be a hard, flat biscuit. She broke it in half, handed me a piece, and started moving again.

"Where does the Grimmerroth come in?" I asked, eager to keep her talking. It's not every millennium that a field archaeologist gets to hear a brand new creation myth. I ached for the loss of my recording equipment. The poetry of the tale of this child god was beautiful. I felt as I had the first time I watched the old glassblower in the museum fashion something wonderful with flame and glowing glass. It had felt like a glittering droplet of truth.

"As she listened to the people she had created, Polnedra became aware of an agony building up in her creation. She did not understand this, but it did not please her, so she asked her father for advice. Milhadron had been watching, but saying nothing, because he believed in letting his child make her own mistakes. But now, when she asked, the mountains rumbled with his voice. 'Child, these creatures are thrice removed from godhood. I see all, and it is. You see all and are delighted. These lesser creatures see all and are crushed by it. You let them contemplate eternity, but cannot give them the minds to encompass it.'

"Polnedra asked her father to fix what she had done. At first he declined, telling her she was responsible for her play-things. She persisted, and he relented. But he did what was wise; instead of raising her playthings to godhood, he instead helped them bear their creation. He took the cosmos from its footings in the Mountains of Darkness and set it spinning. With the spinning came night and day, light and darkness, and so he created Time.

"And he gave to Polnedra's creations the gift of mortality so that they would have no more of eternity than they could bear.

"Polnedra was glad that her creations no longer suffered, but it was not quite the answer she had been hoping for. She withdrew for a while. First, she sulked and threw stones. One hit Rhea and scorched its surface and ended many of her creations. She was sincerely penitent and sought to undo this, but Milhadron had made Time to turn in only one direction.

"She pondered how she could have done better than her father. After a while, she decided that she would impart a larger portion of eternity to her creation. But she didn't want to make a mistake as large as her first, so she made a single creature, and dropped an extraordinary amount of creativity into him. And she called him Glimmer.

"At first this was splendid. Glimmer took up the tools of the smith and hammered fine instruments of iron and copper. He took up the brush of the artist and made creations to elicit joy and love and fear, and any other emotion he cared to essay in any who viewed them. He took up the pen and wrote stories and poems to move the mind and soul of any who read them. He was handsome, and admired, and influential. Polnedra was pleased and manifested in his garden to spend an afternoon in conversation. In this, she made a grave error.

"After the conversation, Glimmer saw what he could have been. Polnedra was young, eternal, beautiful, and could create with the touch of a finger. Flowers dropped from her fingertips as she walked around his garden. For an age after her visit, that garden had flowers found nowhere else in the worlds.

"Glimmer threw himself into creation with a fever, trying to equal his creator. He became stern and uncompromising, striving for ever greater perfection. Yet everything he made he saw only as a shadow of Polnedra's originals. His art became darker, his work at the forge became twisted. His words drove others away. He released demons on the world that killed many. It was then that he became known as Grimmer, first in jest and then in fear.

"His words inspired those who leaned to the darkness themselves. He took delight in whispering in their ears, first in one ear and then another, so that Polnedra's children would first argue, then fight. He made weapons for them to use and invented reasons for them to be used.

"Finally, Polnedra could stand the strife in her creation no longer. She lured Grimmer to a cave in the deepest mountains. She could not reverse Time, but she could stop it in a small area. She touched Grimmer and froze Time in that cavern, turning him into a twisted statue. After he became frozen in his twisted form, he was known thereafter as the Grimmerroth. But Grimmer had suspected her motives and had fashioned a blade that he plunged into her breast and held. As she touched him and froze Time, she froze herself in Time as well.

"To this day, they stand in the darkness, frozen in Time. A few have found this cavern upon occasion. If someone touches them and warms them with a little of their own Time, they are released on the world for a while. The Grimmerroth creates twisted things and twisted people to sow war and destruction on the world. Polnedra tries to rally people to defeat him. Because she is locked in Time and without her powers, each time she faces him she must choose a hero to fight for her against the Grimmerroth."

Books and Stories by Chuck Boeheim

Short Stories

The Ledger
Interaction Region
Void Birds
Viral

Missives from Sellenria (with Daniel Elswit)

Sellenria: The Starship and the Citadel
Sellenria: Jonan's Story (forthcoming)
Sellenria: Gilwyr's Story (forthcoming)

Other Stories

Knots

www.ingramcontent.com/pod-product-compliance
Lightning Source LLC
Chambersburg PA
CBHW022057170626
46808CB00002B/486